What goes around comes around.

Turning over a new leaf isn't easy. Especially when your first task is to plan the wedding of your biggest enemy.

Veronica St. James is determined to set aside her conniving ways and make the wedding a success. Her new boss, Gertie O'Rourke, has put her faith in her, and Veronica won't let her down. Too bad the wedding planning gets complicated when it turns out she'll have to work closely with TJ Flannery, the skinny dishwasher she used to boss around in her last job. Except TJ isn't a skinny dishwasher anymore. He's filled out into a handsome executive, and now he's the one calling the shots.

TJ Flannery has been given a unique opportunity to turn himself around. He's cleaned up his act and is determined that Gertie won't regret the risk she took in hiring him. Keeping the wedding budget on track should be easy for an experienced finance guy like him. What might not be so easy is working with the same feisty blonde that used to bust his chops in his last job.

But when it turns out that someone is trying to sabotage the wedding, Veronica and TJ must work together to soothe the ranting bridezilla and unmask the culprit in order to save Gertie's business as well as their jobs.

WHAT COMES AROUND GOES AROUND

LEIGHANN DOBBS
LISA FENWICK

WHAT COMES AROUND GOES AROUND

·ried. I was just hoping that I could help with this
:ial day."

Veronica vaguely remembered that Marly's mother
almost died of cancer, but a lifesaving treatment
worked on her at the last minute, and she had
·en the cancer. Veronica had even heard a rumor
: her old boss, Jasper Kenney, Marly's fiancé, had
·d for the treatment. But who knew if that was true?

"Marly, you loved everything about this venue for
reception when we took the tour with Gertie a
days ago. What is the issue here? You know we
·'t have much time to get this finalized. Not many
·er venues are available on short notice." Olivia
·nded tired, disappointed, and a bit angry with her
·ghter.

"It's not the building. It's lovely." Marly glanced out
window at the impressive harbor view.

To say that the old mill was lovely was an under-
·ement. Gertie had spent a fortune restoring most
·he building, partitioning it into the offices upstairs
· several rooms for events at the ground level. The
·ms varied in size and offered both indoor and
·door areas with gorgeous water views. Every room
· stunning, with refinished wide-board hardwood
·rs, original antique brick and twenty-foot-high
·ings. The largest room, where Marly's wedding
·uld likely be held, was an indoor-outdoor ballroom

1

There was no way in hell that Veronica St. James
was going to plan a wedding for the woman
sitting across from her.

Never mind that she was trying to turn over that
leaf everyone talks about or that her new boss, Gertie
O'Rourke, was counting on her to make their first
event a success. Veronica and Marly West had a
contentious past that didn't bode well for happy
wedding plans.

"Absolutely not. No. Not her. Anyone but *her*,"
Marly said, echoing Veronica's thoughts as she glared
at her across the sparkling glass conference table.

Good. That should settle it. Marly would refuse,
and they would go on their way. Veronica wouldn't
have to be the one to disappoint Gertie.

She settled back into the plush white leather chair and forced a smile. Looking down at her notepad she caught a glimpse of the chic beige pumps on her feet through the glass tabletop. She'd bought them to go with the off-white Dolce & Gabbana suit she'd splurged on to impress their first client. Of course that was before she knew that client was Marly West. Had she known, she might have worn something different. Like a sweat suit and dirty running shoes.

"Now dear, you know we don't have much of a choice, and Gertie is doing us a big favor." The frail woman beside Marly, who had been introduced as her mother, Olivia, put her hand on Marly's arm. Marly turned to her, her face softening.

Veronica glanced at Gertie, who was looking patiently at Olivia. Did the two women know each other? Veronica wouldn't have been surprised if Gertie had taken the woman under her wing as she did with so many people, including Veronica herself. If Veronica wasn't mistaken, the aqua-and-green silk scarf Olivia had wrapped around her head was one of Gertie's.

"So you girls are already acquainted?" Gertie asked innocently as she pulled her shawl closer together across her chest and eyed Veronica and Marly cautiously. "What a coincidence! It's such a small world, isn't it?"

Neither Veronica nor Marly said a w[...] room fell silent except for the squeaking [...] Gertie's wheelchair as she expertly ma[...] herself across the newly refinished wo[...] slowly moving farther down the table to ge[...] Olivia.

"Olivia, that's certainly a strong-mind[...] lady you have raised!" Gertie patted the bac[...] Olivia's hands as she said it, and the tw[...] exchanged a friendly smile.

"How do you two know each other?[...] could see by the steely glint in Gertie's ey[...] was not going to give up this job easily. [...] she. This job could make or break her ne[...] Veronica felt a pang of guilt. Gertie had go[...] limb by giving her this job. She owed her.

"From the hospital. I volunteer there [...] and then. Olivia and I both love to watch [...] In fact, we spent many a night watching th[...] in her hospital room. Isn't it wonderful [...] thing worked out so well with Olivia's tr[...] that she is in remission? And to think, [...] here with Marly." Gertie removed her [...] Olivia's and placed it on Marly's. "Your [...] get to see you married. I guess not at this [...] the reaction you just had, but that's okay [...] tant thing is that she's here to see her [...]

complete with its own wall fountain and retractable glass wall.

Marly sighed and turned back to the table, her eyes drilling into Veronica's. "It's *her*. She's trouble. I lost my job at Draconia because of her. I mean, I didn't end up losing it, but … well … I mean, I got my job back, but that's not the point. She causes trouble. She did it to me and then to Sarah when she was on that cooking show a few months ago. I just don't want my wedding ruined! What does she know about planning a wedding anyway? Last I knew she was a secretary!"

More guilt. Marly was right. She had done some terrible things in the past. But that was the *old* Veronica. The new Veronica didn't do terrible things to people. The new Veronica was confident, capable, and *nice*. And the new Veronica didn't shy away from a challenge just because it made her feel uncomfortable. Perhaps she should look at this wedding as an opportunity to make things up to Marly. An opportunity for redemption.

Olivia exchanged a raised brow with Gertie. "Honey, are you sure you aren't blowing this out of proportion. I don't remember you telling me anything about losing your job. You might have a case of prewedding jitters. I think you need to reconsider this. The past is water under the bridge. You don't exactly have much time to get this wedding reception planned now, do you? Besides, I trust Gertie. And what she's done to this old mill, well, it's breathtaking! I'm sure Veronica will do her very best to make sure your reception is amazing. I know Gertie would not have given her the position if she wasn't qualified."

"Of course," Gertie chimed in. "Veronica has excellent coordinating skills. And, that is really what wedding receptions are all about—ensuring all of the moving parts flow together seamlessly. It's all about communication and coordination."

Gertie's confidence in her deepened Veronica's guilt. This job was a big step, and this event might be her only chance to prove herself. It might be Gertie's only chance too. Gertie had poured everything into renovating the mill and pulling off a high-society wedding like that of billionaire chief executive officer Jasper Kenney would be a coup that would guarantee a steady stream of future business.

Marly and Jasper's previously chosen venue had been gutted by fire. They chose O'Rourke's as the replacement venue. Another high-profile event would not come as quickly. Not to mention that if Gertie didn't succeed, Veronica would have precious few job prospects.

Her old "partner" in misdeeds, Tanner Durcotte, had blackballed her when she refused to ruin the cooking contest Marly had mentioned. Before Gertie

"There might be another place. Anyplace that doesn't have *her*." Marly's voice wavered uncertainly.

"Every place is booked months in advance, and you only have nine days," Olivia pointed out. "It is only by sheer luck that Gertie has this available. Besides, the room with the water wall and outdoor space is just breathtaking, and I know Edward would love how elegant it is."

Olivia's voice was soft, tired. Veronica saw Marly shoot a concerned glance at her mother. Hopefully she would stop arguing with her and give in. There was no way she'd find a better venue for her wedding at this late date.

Marly stood and started to pace. "This isn't what I had planned on at all. I wanted a small wedding. Elegant, yes. But also simple. Now Edward wants to invite half the city and put on a big show. It's so *not* what I wanted."

"I think you are being overly dramatic. This isn't just *your* wedding, you know," Olivia said matter-of-factly. "You need to learn to compromise with Edward. It will be good practice. Marriage is all about compromise."

"Veronica can work wonders," Gertie assured. "She'll make certain both you and Edward get what you want."

Marly shot Veronica a skeptical glance.

"I'm just glad I'll be around to witness it," Olivia said. "There was a time when I didn't think I'd see my baby married."

Marly turned from the window and looked at her mother with glistening eyes. She put her hand gently on Olivia's shoulder.

Veronica's heart pinched at the obvious love between mother and daughter. Too bad her own mother didn't give a crap about her. She hoped Marly realized how lucky she was to have a good relationship with her mother and to be planning a nice wedding. Veronica was a little envious—she doubted there would be a wedding in her future. Her mother had been right about one thing: men didn't seem to be interested in her for any kind of relationship.

"Okay, Mom. You're right." She said the words softly then turned steely eyes in Veronica's direction, her voice turning hard. "But let me make this clear: this is *my* wedding, and I want *my* instructions to be followed. And no shenanigans. I mean it! If this wedding reception gets messed up because someone screwed around and used Peeps and M&Ms instead of a wedding cake, I will make sure everyone knows how incompetent this business is."

Marly jerked her purse off the chair and stomped out of the room. Olivia raised her brows and mouthed

"Peeps and M&Ms?" before saying a quick goodbye to Gertie and heading off behind Marly.

Veronica watched the empty doorway in silence, half expecting Marly to pop back in with more comments. When she didn't, her eyes moved to Gertie, her apology for the Jucy's comment already forming in her head.

But Gertie didn't reprimand her. Instead she cleared her throat and started to push herself away from the table, pausing to look at Veronica as she did so.

"Well dear, it looks as if we might have ourselves a bridezilla."

2

Veronica practically had to jog to keep up with Gertie. The older woman might be in a wheelchair, but she sure didn't let that slow her down. Good thing she'd started that weight loss and exercise routine, otherwise she'd be out of breath and sweating all over her fancy new suit.

"Good job in the meeting. Sorry that I couldn't bring you up to speed before Marly and Olivia showed up. Things are crazy here, as you know," Gertie said.

"Thanks." Veronica was more relieved than anything that Gertie thought she'd done a good job.

"So you know her and the rest of the people involved?" Gertie glanced up at Veronica quizzically.

"Um… yeah… well, we might not have gotten along so well in the past." Veronica didn't want to think about when she'd worked with Jasper and Marly at Draconia. Of all people, why did her first clients have to bring up such bad memories? Maybe this was a test. She was determined to pass it even if it meant working with her former boss. Would she have to work with Jasper's father, Edward, too? She hadn't exactly been besties with him either.

"Not getting along seems to be a problem with you. But that's not going to stop you from doing a good job, right?"

"Of course not." Another person might have been insulted at Gertie's blunt remark, but after working with her on a televised cooking contest, Veronica knew Gertie's gruff exterior was just that—a facade. Veronica suspected the old woman simply acted mean to hide the fact that she had a heart as big as New England.

"That's my girl. So, then to bring you up to speed, Edward and Marly want different things for the wedding. She wants small and simple, he wants big and fancy. Olivia is happy no matter what, and Jasper is neutral and probably just wants it all to be over with." Gertie maneuvered herself around a can of paint and nodded at the young man dipping a brush into it to touch up the already vibrant white walls.

"Anyway, Marly's original venue was The Marquis. The one that had the bad fire a few weeks ago. Marly has a few things that survived the fire that she will be sending over to us."

"Okay."

"The rest of the items you will either need to buy or get from storage. It's up to you to keep all the parties happy *and* stay within the limited budget." Gertie slowed and leaned toward Veronica. "That Edward sure is a tightwad. With all his money, you'd think he'd spend more on his only son's wedding. But what can you do?"

Veronica shrugged. She didn't have fond memories of Edward and wasn't surprised to find out he was cheap.

"Easy stuff! You can handle that, right? We are under the gun here with only nine days to pull this whole thing off."

"Of course I can handle it, no problem." Veronica hoped Gertie didn't detect the slight tone of panic in her voice. She reminded herself to make sure to actually write things down next time. Things had moved so fast this morning she'd forgotten to take any notes, not that there had been much to take down. It had mostly been about Marly not wanting Veronica to coordinate the wedding.

"That's what I like to hear. The rest of the information is on your desk. I'll check back with you later today." Gertie wheeled off toward her office humming.

Veronica continued down the hall, starting a mental list of everything she needed to do. She was thrilled to have this job. She'd never technically been an "event planner" before, but she had coordinated the entire cooking show where she had met Gertie. Apparently she'd done well enough to impress the old woman.

And before that, as Jasper's assistant, she'd had to organize and coordinate plenty. She could do this. At the show and working for Jasper, she had always been behind the scenes. Now she would actually get credit for her work, whether it was good or bad. She was determined it would be amazing.

Her stomach growled, and she paused briefly, looking around trying to remember where she had seen a small break room that contained a few vending machines. It was her first day working in the building, and she'd barely had time to set up her office before the meeting.

At the top of the stairs, she found the door with "Break Room" on it and pushed it open slowly. The room was immaculate, and Veronica smiled as she pictured Gertie telling whoever was responsible for keeping it clean that it needed to be spotless at all times. Gertie ran a tight ship, and a very clean one at that.

The floor was black tile shot through with white

specks. Cherry-red-lacquered cabinets ran along half of one of the walls. Veronica opened a few of the doors. They were stocked with coffee and teas, ramen noodles, even some cans of tuna fish, in addition to Styrofoam cups and paper plates.

The full-size refrigerator and sink were both much nicer than those in Veronica's apartment. The long, gold-flecked white granite countertop had nary a crumb on it, and housed a toaster, coffee machine, and microwave. Comfortable-looking black leather barstools were situated around four pub tables of dark cherry and granite. The room looked more like something from a glamorous house than an employee break room. Gertie treated her employees well.

She walked toward one of the vending machines, its contents calling out to her from behind the streak-free glass. She pored over the options, her eyes lingering on the familiar brown package of M&Ms that she had chosen hundreds of times before. Not this time. She had lost close to forty pounds after leaving the island where the cooking show had been taped, and she intended on keeping it that way. Even though she wasn't as thin as she had been when she had worked with Marly, she was getting there.

She pushed the buttons for a Peppermint Patty, and it glided effortlessly out of the machine. Peppermint Patties were a good choice—lower in fat and fewer calories. And they were just as satisfying. She picked it up, peeled back the silver wrapping, and took a small bite out of the round minty chocolate.

HARPER SULLIVAN PEEKED over the railing at the top of the stairway, making sure that no one was on their way up to the break room. She had discreetly followed Veronica upstairs to meet her. She was curious after all the things she'd heard from her Uncle Tanner. Could the woman really be *that* bad?

Harper loved her uncle more than anyone. He was all she had left, and after everything he'd been through, she knew she should cut him some slack. But she also knew he could be a bit dramatic.

She cautiously pushed open the door to the break room. Her eyes fell on Veronica standing in front of the vending machine, and she tried to feign surprise.

"Oh, hi! Sorry to barge in. I'm Harper, nice to meet you." She extended her hand and waited while Veronica juggled her cell phone and a Peppermint Patty, so she could shake hands.

"Hi, I'm Veronica. Veronica St. James. It's nice to meet you."

Harper smiled, giving Veronica a quick once-over. Uncle Tanner had said she was stick thin and sickly looking. Was this the right Veronica? This woman was curvy and definitely didn't look sickly.

She wore a top-notch designer suit, and her dark blond hair, which had been pulled up into a ponytail on top, fell past her shoulders. She had high cheekbones and large velvety-brown eyes. Her face was a bit thin. Maybe that's what Uncle Tanner had meant.

"This is a great break room, huh? Gertie went all out on it, that's for sure. Those cabinets are stocked with coffee pods for the Keurig, and there's a bunch of tea in the other ones." Veronica pointed to the wall of cabinets as Harper looked around.

"So how many people work here?" Veronica asked.

"Did you just start?" Harper pretended she didn't already know it was the woman's first day.

"Yeah. First day."

"I haven't been here that long either. Well, I guess none of us have, but it seems there are a lot of employees. I'm not sure how many exactly. I'm psyched we have our first wedding. I heard the bride is some fashion designer and the groom is her boss, or something weird like that. Her original venue burned down two weeks ago. Can you imagine that happening?" Harper clenched her fist, digging her nails into her palm to stop the nervous babble streaming from her mouth. She was actually pretty introverted, so talking to a stranger like this was a bit out of her comfort zone. Still, it had to be done if she wanted to keep her promise to her uncle.

"Yeah, it's definitely going to be a challenge to throw a wedding together in nine days, but I'm sure we can do it. How do you know Gertie?" Veronica asked.

"Oh, I work downstairs."

Veronica's face twisted a bit, and Harper immediately knew that she needed to say something more to avoid answering her question in further detail. Her uncle had pulled some strings to make sure she'd been hired to take inventory and sort through all of the crap Gertie had bought from other venues, as well as be a gofer. But she didn't want Veronica to know that.

"So what do you do here anyway? I saw you earlier in a meeting, I think?"

"I'm the event planner. I work with the bride and groom, plan things out, you know." Veronica crumpled up her candy wrapper and tossed it into the trash.

"Oh, cool! So you get to plan all the stuff, huh? So you aren't worried about the wedding? I mean, having to pull things together so fast and all," Harper asked.

"I think it will be fine. It'll be a lot of work, but Gertie is counting on me. Besides, I know some of the stuff that the bride wants survived the fire at the other place, so at least I won't be starting from scratch. She can still use the same photographer and band, so I won't have to deal with that."

"You probably have to have a lot of meetings and work pretty closely given the limited amount of time." Harper hoped it didn't sound as though she was fishing for information.

Veronica nodded. "The bride, Marly, is supposed to come by the day after tomorrow to look at a few things Gertie has in-house, like the linens and centerpieces. I just hope we have something she likes."

Veronica spoke as if she didn't like Marly that much. Hadn't Uncle Tanner said that Marly and Veronica were good friends?

"Yeah, people can get worked up over this stuff. Even if they are normally really nice," Harper said, hoping her comment would entice Veronica to say more.

"Yeah, and when they aren't nice to begin with..." Veronica let the sentence trail off, apparently realizing she'd said too much.

But Harper had heard what she needed. Maybe Uncle Tanner had been right about her.

Harper leaned toward Veronica conspiratorially and lowered her voice. "I know. Some girls just turn into total bitches, especially if they are prone to that. And here I heard that the couple was like some power couple or something. You'd think that would make anyone act nice."

"They are. The perfect power couple. But with a strict budget. But not strict enough that she couldn't drop the dough to design her own wedding gown with one of those over-the-top boutique wedding shops."

"Well, that's one less thing you'll have to deal with." Harper had an idea. "Is that the shop on East Lowe Street?"

Veronica scrunched up her face. "I'm not sure. Maybe. Anyway, I gotta run. It was great to meet you. I'm sure we'll see each other around."

Harper watched Veronica leave. She'd seemed nice at first, but Uncle Tanner was right. Veronica definitely didn't seem happy for Marly. What kind of a mean person wouldn't be happy about helping to plan a friend's wedding?

Then again, given what had happened with Harper's own wedding, she could see how weddings in general could make one cranky. Maybe Veronica had a sob story like Harper's.

She glanced down at her phone, her chest constricting when she saw there was no text yet from Tanner. Her parents had been killed when she was just a toddler, and Uncle Tanner and Aunt Emily had opened their home and their hearts to her. She owed him, but she wasn't so sure about some of the things he'd asked her to do here.

She sat on one of the barstools, family duty warring with her sense of right and wrong. But then she remembered how despondent her uncle had been when his fashion company, Theorim Designs, had failed. That company had been the only thing that had pulled him out of the depression he'd sunk into after Aunt Emily died.

Tanner had told her that Veronica and Marly were responsible for the company failing. She didn't know what they had done to cause the company to collapse, but they both deserved what they were about to get.

3

Back in her office, Veronica kicked herself for opening her big mouth in front of that girl, Harper. Lucky she hadn't actually said all of the bad things she'd been thinking about Marly in her head out loud. It wasn't smart to bad-mouth the client, even if the person you were talking to seemed sympathetic.

She'd have to be careful about what she said to people. She needed to act professionally and didn't want to do anything to jeopardize this job. Especially when it came with this nice corner office. As a secretary, she'd never had her own office. She'd always been relegated to a desk outside the boss's plush digs. But the office Gertie had given her was nice and, even though not very large, it was bright and cheery, with rows of windows on two of the walls.

The office furniture wasn't too shabby either. Like everything Gertie did, it was top-notch, right down to the contemporary glass-top, cross-base desk and turquoise accessories. Gertie had thought of everything—an ergonomic desk chair and two white leather club chairs for guests. Like everything else in the mill, the floor was hardwood, most of which was covered with a vibrant turquoise-and-silver rug. There was even a large potted plant, some kind of ficus tree or something. Veronica just hoped she'd remember to water it. Or did Gertie have someone who did that?

She sat down and opened the file for the wedding that Gertie had left on the desk. Gertie had made it very clear to her earlier that morning that no money could be spent until Veronica put together a budget and got it approved by the finance guy.

Grabbing a highlighter, she started to go through the items. Hm... this wouldn't be so easy. Marly wanted a very simple reception, almost too simple. Edward wanted the opposite. And Edward was paying for the whole thing but wanted to spend no more than sixty-thousand! Who could pull off a wedding like this for that small amount?

Veronica wondered if The Marquis had been able to arrange a wedding with that budget. Maybe they'd burned their own venue down in frustration. It was her problem now, though, and she needed to ensure both Marly and Edward were happy.

Edward wanted lobster and filet for dinner options. Marly had asked that it be chicken or fish. Edward wanted a champagne fountain. Marly stated "absolutely no champagne fountains." Oy, this was starting to get stressful. She would have to tread very lightly to ensure she didn't upset either of them.

Her hand automatically reached into her pocket, and she fumbled around for her lip balm, applying it without even thinking. She'd picked up the new habit when she had started to diet. Any time she started feeling anxious or nervous, she applied the balm instead of reaching for something to eat.

She made a list of Edward's criteria for the reception on one side of a piece of paper and a list of Marly's on the other side. They had actually agreed on a few things, and she crossed those off. Now she just needed to figure out how to make them meet in the middle with the rest and stick to Edward's budget.

She decided to tackle one of the larger costs first, the flowers. Marly wanted simple and nothing flashy, too bright, or bold. Edward wanted a variety. They had already met with a florist months ago when the original venue was booked, but it looked as if nothing had been finalized for the actual arrangements.

Edward had placed a deposit with the florist.

According to the notes, O'Rourke's would be paying the remainder because Gertie wanted her venue to be all-inclusive. That meant Veronica had to stick with the same vendor. Too bad, because she knew they were expensive. Then again, she didn't have to use them for all the florals. Why not use the deposit money for the bouquets and make up some of the budget on the centerpieces and the rest?

She conducted a few searches on her computer for photos of floral arrangements and came up with an idea for the flowers: lavender roses paired with daisies. Simple yet elegant. And fairly inexpensive. Marly had made it clear she didn't want a lot of different flowers. Edward had insisted there be a variety. Technically two could be considered a variety. At least she hoped she could make Edward see it that way.

Next up, the special place cards Edward wanted for each table. This should be easy. A simple white china with gold lettering. That would satisfy Marly's wish for something simple. Maybe Gertie even had something suitable on hand. She'd have to get down to the storage area to check. Worst case, she could order them and have the delivery expressed on short notice, though doing so would drive up the cost.

The longer she worked on the proposal, the more optimistic she felt. In fact, she felt downright happy, something she hadn't allowed herself to feel in a long time.

Helping Marly and Edward almost felt... right. Is this what it felt like to be a nice person? Veronica wasn't sure. She'd spent most of her life angry and bitter, always plotting someone's downfall.

But she didn't want the crappy childhood she'd had to define her life anymore. Gertie had shown her that it didn't have to be that way. She'd shown her that no matter what your limitations, you could succeed, and that no matter how many times others tried to knock you down, you could get back up.

For the first time in Veronica's life, she felt pride in herself. It sucked that there was so much stress given the time frame, but she knew she could do it. Gertie wouldn't have hired her if she didn't think Veronica could pull it off, and she was going to make sure she did!

She got back to work with renewed determination, transferring her scrawled-out numbers onto her computer and adding up the figures carefully. Once she finished, she leaned back in her chair and rechecked the budget, a feeling of joy bubbling up inside her. This just might work. She had compromised on a few things but had given Edward and Marly most of what they each requested while not spending a penny more than Edward stipulated.

She hit the print key, then stood up slowly and stretched. Walking over to the printer, she grabbed the papers, shoved them into a folder, and wrote "West/Kenney Wedding" on it. She wanted to take this to finance immediately for review and approval so that she could start ordering. There was no time to waste.

She hurried into the hall and then stopped short. Now, where was his office again? Gertie had been moving so fast when she had shown her around earlier that morning that it had all been a big blur. She knew the office was on the same floor, so maybe she could find it.

She walked slowly past each door, stopping when she saw one that had a "Finance" sign on it, with the name "TJ Flannery" under it. That's kind of an unprofessional name—TJ—she thought. Whatever. As long as he knew how to crunch numbers, it didn't matter what he called himself.

She knocked.

No answer.

She glanced at her watch. Dang! It was almost six thirty. The guy was probably gone for the day.

Didn't that figure! She needed that approval pronto, and here the guy was leaving work early. Okay, well, it wasn't actually early, but... didn't he know they had a looming deadline for this important client? Hopefully Gertie hadn't hired a slacker to take care of the finances. That would make Veronica's job more difficult.

With a sigh, she placed the paperwork in a hanging wall file holder next to the door and left, satisfied with her first day on the job. She sure hoped this TJ guy started work early.

4

Tanner Durcotte ended his call and sipped his coffee, enjoying the view of the busy New York street from the premier table in one of his restaurants. He liked watching the people scurry by, always in a hurry to get to work. They were like ants, the way they ran along, heads down, occasionally bumping into each other and continuing along their way.

When he had first opened his restaurants, he had considered offering breakfast, but he knew that the majority of these city people liked a quick bite for breakfast, and he preferred his customers stay a while and enjoy their meals, making it more of an experience. It was just as well. He liked having the place all to himself in the morning anyway. Watching the crowd made him feel less lonely for some reason.

He opened the manila folder on the table in front of him and looked at the drawings he had received the day before. Nice. Very nice, actually. The gown was impressive, eye-catching but not gaudy. Its sleek lines and long train were rare these days, and he almost felt bad with what he was about to do. Almost.

He slapped the folder shut and looked back out at the street, the sleek image of the gown still on his mind. If anyone would recognize a good design, he would. He used to own Theorim Designs, one of the premier fashion houses in New York City. *Used to.*

His fist clenched, his face burned, and his chest tightened with bad memories of how that traitor Marly West had screwed him over and driven him out of business.

"Everything okay, Mr. Durcotte?" The waitress, Kyla, appeared at his elbow with a pot of coffee and a look of concern. When had he started to become familiar with the names of the help? He must be getting soft in his old age, just as his niece Harper always teased.

Thoughts of Harper calmed him. She was the one bright spot in his life. So sweet despite the raw deal life had handed her. Tanner had always tried to shelter her from the realities of life. He didn't want her to suffer as he had. His fist relaxed, and he took a deep breath.

"Yes, everything is fine." He smiled and nodded at his cup. She filled it before leaving.

That mess with Theorim had a silver lining. It had given him time to focus on his restaurants. He was lucky the restaurants were thriving, as that all could have gone south due to another traitor—Veronica St. James.

But karma had a way of coming around, and now he'd have a chance to get back at both of them. What a rare opportunity! He should have been overjoyed, but for some reason the victory did not taste very sweet.

He glanced down at his phone on the table. It had gone into sleep mode, and the photo of his late wife, Emily, beamed up at him, making him doubt everything he was about to do. Deep down, he knew Emily would not have approved of many of the things he'd done since she'd died. But Emily wasn't here. She didn't know how much he'd been hurt.

He punched in his code, and her face disappeared. Maybe it was time he replaced that screen saver anyway.

He texted Harper to ask her to make a call for him and relay what he needed her to say. He had a momentary pang of indigestion. It wasn't fair using Harper to do his dirty work, but he had no one else. Besides, *he* was on the side of right. He would never ask Harper to do anything really bad... just a few little favors.

He settled back in his chair and looked out the window again, a smile firmly planted on his face.

TJ RUMMAGED through the cabinet for the dark-roast coffee pods. He always started his day with as much caffeine as possible, and today he was going to need plenty. He'd have his work cut out for him with the budget for the wedding. Not that he minded. After years on the streets, being back at work in a real job and having a real purpose again was a godsend.

He popped the coffee pod into the machine and placed his mug beneath the spigot. The machine whirred to life and poured his coffee out as he grabbed some milk from the refrigerator. He poured a small amount into his mug and stirred it with a spoon then took a sip. Delicious. He washed off the spoon and headed back to his office.

Settling into his chair, he scoured the proposal that had been shoved into his in-tray after hours. His eyes caught on the name of the person who had filled it out.

Veronica St. James. How did he know that name? It sounded so familiar.

He took another sip of coffee and leaned back in his chair, his brow furrowed as he thought. He hadn't met many people in the past year. In fact, he'd avoided people. Except for Gertie, of course. She was different. Wait… that's why the name was familiar. Veronica St. James was that blonde from the cooking contest who had done nothing but yell and boss everyone around.

How in the world had she ended up here? Had to be Gertie's doing. Gertie had a way of collecting people and giving them a second chance. That's how TJ had ended up here, a chance for which he'd be eternally grateful.

Did Veronica need a second chance? TJ didn't know much about her. It's not as if they'd been friends.

A smile spread across TJ's face as he remembered the first time he had met Veronica. He had been clean for about a year when he'd ended up on the tropical island of Namara. Not that he could afford to jet away to an island, but the people he owed money to had threatened his family. He'd borrowed money and pulled in some favors to change his last name and get away, so he could keep his parents and sister safe until he earned enough to pay his debt.

He'd been working as a dishwasher on the set of a cooking show when Veronica had barged into the kitchen and demanded that he clean twice the amount of cookware that was needed. That was just the first of many times she'd wreaked havoc in the kitchen. The rest of the kitchen staff had called her "Attila" behind her back.

She was arrogant, bossy, and dismissive. Another guy would have been pissed, but TJ was easygoing and generally happy most of the time. He'd recognized something in her that made him sympathetic. It took a lot to get him ruffled, and her constant outbursts only amused him, which seemed to make her angrier, which amused him even more.

Funny how life could turn the tables. On the cooking show, Veronica had been the one calling the shots, but now *he* was calling them, at least in regard to the budget. And the proposal she'd handed in for the wedding was far too high.

He reached for his calculator and started to mark up the file with a red pen, circling and crossing out numbers as he moved down the page.

He had changed a lot in the six months that had passed since he'd been on the cooking show. He wondered if Veronica would even recognize him. Probably not. He doubted she'd paid much attention to him. He'd simply been a skinny dishwasher she could boss around. He was sure she didn't even know his name. On the island, she hadn't bothered to ask. She'd usually been too busy barking orders at him.

After the cooking show wrapped, he'd left the island and returned to New York. He'd paid off his debt and even had money left over to help him get a fresh start.

He'd stayed in a halfway house for a while, but had given up his room to a scrawny kid who would never have survived on the streets. TJ knew how to survive, so he'd bought a cheap tent and set up at one of his old haunts under a bridge. It wouldn't be for long, just until he could get enough money for the first and last month's rent all apartment owners demanded.

Even though he had a degree in accounting, his skills were rusty, and he had a big gap in his resume. He got a job at a small furniture company working in the delivery department. The pay wasn't much, but the tips were all cash, and the job didn't require him to dress up, so the fact he showed up in jeans and tattered shirts really didn't matter. The long hours hadn't bothered him and had the added benefit of building his muscles much more than a gym membership would have. Plus the long work hours meant less time in the tent.

He'd been working toward a plan. Get a steady job. Get a place. Take some classes to get back into accounting. Get his life back together. Then reestablish contact with his family. It was this last one that was most important.

But then things had gone terribly wrong. His chest tightened with panic at the memory of waking in the middle of the night trapped in the smoke-filled tent. The stench of burning plastic, the terrifying crackling as the flames engulfed the tent. TJ had tried to battle his way out, but the tent had collapsed in on him, covering him in a scorching blanket of flames and melting nylon.

TJ's breath came in shallow pants as he heard the sound of his own screams. He rubbed the scars on the backs of his hands, his eyes seeing only the blistering orange sheets of fire.

"Everything okay, doll?" a familiar voice dragged TJ back to the present, and he looked up to see Gertie smiling at him.

"Everything's great, Gertie." He managed a tight smile.

"That's my boy! I'm here all day if you need me, doll!" she said, wheeling herself away.

TJ's smile widened. He loved that crazy old woman. She'd given him a chance many wouldn't have, and he was determined to make sure this first event was a huge success.

Funny, the tent fire had been the thing that had allowed Gertie to find him. Apparently she'd been searching for him for a while, wanting to offer him this job, but because he'd given up his spot at the halfway house, she couldn't find him there, and his delivery job was under-the-table. The fire had landed him in the hospital, and that's how Gertie found him.

If it hadn't been for Gertie giving him this job, TJ didn't know where he'd be now. But now all the bad days were behind him. His debt was paid. He had an apartment and had even reconnected with his family, though his sister was still coming to grips with the fact that he'd stayed away so long. He still couldn't make her understand it had all been to *protect* her.

Life was looking up for him for the first time in a long time.

He finished marking up Veronica's proposal and dialed her extension, disguising his voice a little when she answered. He wanted to mess with her a bit. That had always been fun on the island. He asked her to come to his office to review what she had submitted and hung up, quickly running his hands through his short hair and straightening his shirt.

A few seconds later, someone tapped on his open door, and he looked up, taken aback. She looked different from when he had last seen her. She'd lost weight and now he could see she had curves in all the right places. Her hair color was a bit toned down from the harsh bright blond, and her tresses fell across her shoulders like silk, not frizzy and haggard as on the island.

She hesitated in the doorway. He thought he saw a

slight flicker of recognition in her eyes, but he could tell that she couldn't quite place him.

TJ stood. "Hi, I'm TJ. Come on in. Grab a seat. He held out his hand, and they shook. Her skin was soft but her handshake firm. He motioned for her to sit across from him, and then he sat back down, pulling the cuffs of his white button-down shirt over the scars on the backs of his hand self-consciously. "I just wanted to go over the proposal with you. You did a good job, but it's too much money."

A crease formed between Veronica's brows as she eyed the red-marked proposal on his desk. He waited for her to lash out at him as she had done on the island, but instead she took a deep breath and sat back in the chair.

"Could you give me some specifics on what's too much? As you can see, the bottom line is exactly the amount of the budget."

"Right, the *total* budget, but that needs to include the band and photographer. You need to come in way below that." TJ pointed at a line on the sheet. "Here's an example. These flowers… they're way too much. We have agreements with local florists. The one you are using isn't on the list, so maybe that's why it's pricier."

"The florist was already agreed upon by the bride, and the groom's father gave a nonrefundable deposit.

They are providing all the flowers for the church service, so I had no choice but to use them for the bouquets as well. Otherwise we risk the flowers being totally different quality," Veronica explained firmly.

"Aren't all flowers the same? I mean, it's an additional three thousand dollars to go with that florist. It might seem small in the whole scheme of things, but it's actually a decent chunk of change. And again, it's just flowers." TJ kept his face impassive even though he could see his words had hit a nerve.

He had to admit he was kind of getting a kick out of messing with her just like on the island, but the truth was, he did need to keep things within budget for Gertie. And who cared if the flowers came from a different florist? A daisy was a daisy, wasn't it?

"What? *Just* flowers? No, not all flowers are the same! Some florists are really crappy and don't use the freshest stock. Do we really want to risk having wilted, dying flowers for our first wedding reception?" Veronica shot back, defending her choice. Suddenly her eyes narrowed. "Wait a minute. I know you. How do I know you? The island! You're that dishwasher!"

TJ laughed and held up his hands. "Guilty as charged."

"What are you doing here?" Veronica demanded, looking around the room as if she thought she might be getting punked.

"Gertie hired me."

"A dishwasher? To do accounting?" Her voice sounded incredulous, but as she eyed him, TJ could tell that she was starting to see he was much more than a dishwasher.

"I'm not really a dishwasher. I was down on my luck back then. Gertie befriended me and knew my real story. You know how Gertie likes to champion the underdog."

Veronica's left brow shot up, but she didn't pry into his background. She simply said, "Yes, I do."

"Anyway, Gertie knew that I have a degree in finance. She needed a finance guy here, so she looked me up. I'm grateful she did and want to make sure her new endeavor is a success." TJ sat back in his chair. "How did you end up here?"

"Same way. Gertie liked my work on the cooking show and offered me a job. I'm also grateful and want to make sure her new endeavor is a success."

TJ caught a glimpse of the Veronica he knew from the island in the way she agreed with him but made it sound like a challenge. "Good then. We're on the same page. And now that you've explained the flowers, I get it. But if you want to keep the flowers, you have to trim somewhere else. There are other expenses in the background besides what you have on this page, and Gertie was very clear about the bottom line. We have to stick to it. You need to come in below fifty thousand."

Veronica held his gaze for a second then looked down at the papers and nodded as she scooped them up and stood. "I'll rework it and get this back to you as soon as possible. I know Edward is in a rush to have the numbers finalized."

TJ stared at the doorway for a few seconds after she left. Apparently he wasn't the only one who had changed since the cooking show. And even though Veronica hadn't been as argumentative or bossy, he had the distinct feeling that things were about to get a lot more interesting now that they would be working together.

5

Veronica marched down the hall toward her office, her cheeks burning. She reached into her pocket for her lip balm, swiping it haphazardly across her lips as she mumbled to herself.

"Really? The dishwasher is now the finance guy, and he's making her redo all of her work? Is this real life?"

But he wasn't really a dishwasher. He'd been a finance guy the whole time. So then how had he ended up working as a dishwasher on the cooking show? He must have done something really bad. But Veronica trusted Gertie, and if Gertie thought he would do a good job, then Veronica had to trust that he would. TJ *had* been a hard worker on the island.

TJ. So that was his name. Veronica felt ashamed

she'd never even thought to ask back on the island. But that was the old Veronica. The new Veronica treated people better. Like not prying into his personal life to find out what, exactly, he'd done, even though she was dying to know.

She passed the girl that she'd met in the break room yesterday, Harper, but didn't stop to talk to her. She didn't have time for chitchat right now because she had to redo this stupid proposal.

She plopped herself down at her desk and spread the paperwork TJ had given her across her desk. She hunched over the papers, working quickly to cross off items and jot notes. It would have been nice if Gertie had mentioned that she didn't have the entire budget for the things on her list. Oh well, she'd figure it out. She really needed to get down to the storage area and see what Gertie had in stock.

As she worked, her thoughts drifted back to TJ. He'd changed since she'd last seen him on the island. Then he had been scrawny; now not so much. He'd filled out in a good way. The scraggly beard was gone, and his hair was cut short. With his bangs out of his face, his blue eyes were really noticeable—as was his ever-present, annoyingly cheerful attitude.

Why was he always so damn happy anyway? He had mentioned being down on his luck when he had worked on the island. Could have fooled her. He always seemed to be smiling and laughing. Was it really possible to always be happy? Maybe she should try it.

But not today. Today she had to get this proposal finished. She didn't have time to waste trying to figure out how to smile and act happy all the time.

She couldn't order any of the items she needed for Marly's wedding until TJ approved this stupid thing, and with only eight days until the wedding, she needed every second she could get. She didn't want to drive up delivery costs by having to overnight things.

She logged onto her computer and immediately got an error message. What? She entered her password again, slowly typing it out while mumbling to herself. It worked, but now there was another error message on the screen.

Great. The internet connection wasn't working. Fine. The file is on the in-house server, so no big deal.

Wait... nope... can't access that either.

What is going on?

Veronica's anxiety soared, and she hit the keys harder, retyping the password. Nothing. Dammit! This proposal needs to be approved today before Gertie meets with Edward!

She grabbed the computer monitor and shook it. Maybe a wire was loose. Nope, no change. Just as she was about to kick the PC tower her cell phone rang.

It was her mother. Great! She hesitated, took a deep breath, and then pressed the answer button.

"Hi, Mom." She tried to force a cheerful note into her voice. She hadn't spoken with her mother in a few weeks and could only imagine why she'd call without a reason. They usually spoke only on holidays or birthdays. Or when her mother needed something or wanted to start an argument.

"I haven't heard from you lately. Is everything okay? I didn't know if maybe you'd been ill. You know, from your weight gain. All that added stress on your body, it's just so bad for it."

Apparently this was one of the times she wanted to argue. Veronica slumped in her chair, the familiar feeling of inadequacy creeping over her accompanied by an immediate craving for M&Ms. She fished the lip balm from her pocket instead and mashed it onto her lips.

"I'm fine, Mom. I lost almost all the weight after I left my job on the island, remember? I feel great. And I have a new job. I'm the event manager for O'Rourke Signature Events. You know, the huge mill next to the river that was remodeled?"

Veronica mashed on more lip balm, waiting for her mother's response, cursing the tiny spark of hope that flickered in her chest. Maybe she would actually be happy for her for once. Technically the word "manager" wasn't in her job title, but she could fib a little. And the local newspaper had published a small article on Gertie and the mill's restoration. Maybe her mother had read it.

"What? What do you mean 'event manager'? So you're basically like a hostess? Well, that's interesting."

Veronica let out a heavy sigh, the spark of hope extinguished.

"No, Mom. I'm not a hostess. I'm responsible for planning weddings and parties, things like that. On a very large scale. The wedding I'm planning now is going to cost well over sixty thousand dollars."

"Oh. Well, that sounds like something anyone could do. How hard could it be?"

Veronica struggled to control the anger that was rising up. It was always the same with her mother. Never thin enough. Never smart enough. Her jobs were never anything to be proud of. She wished she could be more like TJ. He would probably just laugh and start whistling. She smeared more balm on her lips.

"Really, Mom, could you maybe be happy for me just *once*? Possibly encourage me even, instead of always being so negative?" It was only with great effort that she kept her tone even.

"Veronica, you're such a crybaby! Maybe if you had a *real* job I'd be happy for you!" her mother shot back.

That did it. Veronica tossed the lip balm on the desk, stood, and yelled into the phone. "I'm sick of your attitude, Mom. This *is* a real job, and maybe if you paid even the least bit of attention to anything I've done in life, you'd be supportive instead of being such a *bitch*!"

She ended the call, plopped down in her chair, and stared at the blank screen on her computer. Even though she knew she should have exerted more control, the yelling had released her frustrations. Still, the dreaded feelings of childhood inadequacy remained. What if her mother was right and she couldn't pull this wedding off?

No. The old Veronica thought that way. The new Veronica got things done. She could do this. If only she could get the stupid computer to work.

HARPER PEELED herself away from the brick wall where she'd been eavesdropping near Veronica's office. She couldn't believe someone would talk to their mother like that! She'd even called her a bitch.

Harper's eyes stung as she hurried down the hall. How many times had she wished her own mother was around for something as simple as a phone call? But her mother had died when she was a baby. Even though Aunt Emily was loving and kind and tried to fill her shoes, it just wasn't the same.

Harper had never gotten the chance to talk to her mother on the phone or do any of the things that most daughters took for granted. If she had, she never would have been so disrespectful. Veronica must really be an awful person, just as her Uncle Tanner had said.

Harper was glad she found out. She was starting to feel bad about messing with computer cables while Veronica was meeting with the hot finance guy.

She hadn't done anything permanent. Veronica would most likely be able to fix it, but at least it slowed her down a bit. That was just a little bump in the road. Harper had a massive road block coming soon, thanks to her instructions from Uncle Tanner.

Squeak. Squeak.

Shoot! Gertie was coming. Harper ducked into an empty office. She was supposed to be taking inventory in the musty basement of the items Gertie had bought from a caterer that had gone out of business. She didn't want Gertie to see her up here. It wouldn't be good to call attention to herself or have anyone wonder why she was on a floor she shouldn't be on.

She waited until the squeaking stopped before peering out into the hallway. Gertie must have gone into Veronica's office. Hopefully she'd be in there for a while.

Harper hurried out into the hall and toward the elevator. She needed to work fast to complete the inventory. Even though this wasn't a position she would stay at, she still wanted to do a good job. It wouldn't do to get fired before she accomplished her mission. Uncle Tanner was counting on her.

6

Veronica was on the floor under her desk concentrating on trying to figure out if the octopus of computer cables were all plugged in properly when Gertie's voice startled her. She jumped, smacking her head on the bottom of the desk. "Ouch."

"What's going on in here? What the heck are you doing down there?"

Veronica backed out, rubbing her head. "I'm checking the cables. Something's wrong with my computer. I'm trying to get the proposal done so TJ can approve it and I can get the ball rolling on Marly's wedding. Again." As soon as she said the last part she wished she hadn't. Gertie didn't need to know that she had come in way over the budget and that TJ had returned the proposal to her covered in red ink.

Gertie's eyes narrowed and her head craned forward. "What is that all over your lips?"

Veronica swiped at her lips, coming away with globs of lip balm on the back of her hand. She might have put too much on during the phone conversation with her mother.

"Just some lip balm."

Gertie's gaze moved to the computer. "So you're still working on the proposal?"

Veronica nodded, her gut tightening.

"Huh. That Edward is a real prize. He's trying to run this wedding like it's a company. Telling me when he wants the proposal and that he expects better pricing as this is our first event. Pffft. Typical rich cheapskate!"

"Tell me about it." Veronica knew how cheap Edward could be.

"I mean, hell, his company doesn't even have fashions for wheelchair users. Try sitting in a chair sixteen hours a day with normal pants on! The zippers and buttons digging into your waist. My stomach looks like a damn roadmap at night when I get undressed for bed! And sleeves! I've had so many damn sleeves get caught in the spokes of these wheels!" Gertie paused, a thoughtful look coming over her face. "Humph. Maybe I should talk to him about that. In the meantime, he just added fifty people to the guest list, so now he's giving us—and by *us* I mean you—until tomorrow night for the proposal to be finalized."

"Fifty people?" Veronica reached for her lip balm, then stopped herself. She already had to cut ten grand off her original proposal, and she'd spent hours on that. Now she needed to not only cut down the original proposal, but do it with an extra fifty people? How was that even possible? She plopped down in her office chair, a feeling of despair sweeping over her.

"Chin up, sunshine. I wouldn't have given you this job if I didn't think you could do it! Even pulling a wedding together in less than two weeks is possible. You did great stuff on the show. Think of this as a challenge! Are you going to let Edward win? I know you can come in under his ridiculous budget."

Veronica's heart warmed at Gertie's pep talk. She needed it, especially after that demoralizing call with her mother. "Of course I can… just as soon as I get this computer working again."

Gertie wheeled herself to the wall and leaned over near where the cable came out.

"Hm. Dear, this is most likely the culprit of your computer problem." Gertie held up a crimped cable. "I'll have Rob from IT bring you a new one. In the meantime, hopefully this will do." She straightened out the cable with her long, thin fingers and plugged it back into the wall. "It's the wire from the wall to your computer that's the issue. Next time just call Rob."

"Gertie! There you are. I..." Edward Kenney appeared outside the door, his frown focused on Veronica. "Miss St. James?"

Veronica's stomach dropped. She hadn't seen him since she'd been fired from Draconia more than a year ago. He looked the same, tall, dark, and moody. Back then he'd always complimented her work and even sided with her against Marly, but when things had gone bad, he'd turned on her.

"Oh, have you two met? This is Veronica St. James. She's your wedding planner. Actually, she's my event person." Gertie waved her hand between Veronica and Edward. "And this is Edward Kenney, father of the groom."

Edward's lips pursed. "No, I don't think so. She isn't planning my Jasper's wedding. She's actually..."

"Yes, she is." Gertie cut Edward off. "Veronica is one of the best in the industry." She threw a wink at Veronica.

"The best in the industry? I don't know about that. However, I do know that she worked for me and..." Edward stared at Veronica, as if he wasn't quite positive she was the same woman who had worked for him.

"Then you know how good she is at what she does,

don't you? I mean a seasoned executive like you wouldn't hire someone who was incompetent, right? You'd only hire the best," Gertie said, cutting him off again as she strategically ushered him out of the room. "Let's go to my office."

Edward glanced back at Veronica over his shoulder as they left. "Well, if you insist that she's the best and Jasper's wedding will be managed correctly, I will take your word for it. I'm trusting you, Gertie."

"Of course, of course. Now, about that fashion line of yours. I think wheelchair fashions could be a good niche, pants and shirts..."

Veronica turned back to the computer. Gertie's fix had worked! Good, because now that she'd seen Edward, Veronica was more determined than ever to nail down this budget.

Her determination didn't come from spite, though. That would have been the *old* Veronica. The new Veronica wanted to nail the budget so that Gertie's business would succeed and to prove to herself to Gertie—and maybe even a little to her mother and Edward—that she was more competent than ever.

7

The next morning, Veronica made herself her sixth cup of coffee, or was it her seventh? She'd worked late into the night and then had returned early that morning to put the finishing touches on the proposal. Good thing there was a Keurig in the break room or she'd probably be asleep under her desk right now.

She'd kept the Keurig and the vending machine busy—the stain in her coffee mug and the pile of silver candy wrappers in her trash barrel were proof. Eating Peppermint Patties for dinner and breakfast probably wasn't the best idea, but it would have to do for now. She'd work it off by taking the stairs as much as she could.

She looked over the proposal for what she hoped would be the last time. Adding fifty people to the guest list hadn't driven the cost up as much as she'd feared. She finagled the appetizers around, cut one of the vegetable sides, and managed to reduce costs accordingly. She'd spend half of her night reconfiguring the layout of the reception room to fit an additional seven tables and floating bar.

She'd added outdoor seating under a large tent to the proposal. This wouldn't cost anything as they already had a tent in-house, and she needed the extra space because the tables for the fifty extra guests would have lessened the space for the dance floor.

Marly had emphasized that there would be a lot of dancing at the reception, and Veronica wanted to make sure she got what she wanted. Veronica had even added a second dance floor under the tent, with two floating bars at either end and some bar-height tables set up for conversation. Because the glass end wall in the reception room opened, the space would flow into the tent.

She gnawed on her bottom lip as she worked on the graphic representation of the new setup. Marly was really going to like it. At least Veronica hoped she would. It's what Veronica would have chosen for her own reception. Despite the problems Veronica and Marly had had in the past, she genuinely wanted the wedding to be successful. Ha! Imagine that? Veronica hoping one of her former enemies would have a dream wedding. She really was growing.

She knew Edward and Marly would most likely fuss over the room being set up differently than it had originally been shown to them, which was why she'd done the extra work of creating the graphic showing the layout with the new setup and tent. She'd even double-checked the forecast. There was no indication of rain.

Satisfied that everything was in order, she hit the send key, emailing the proposal to TJ, and then printed a copy. As she basked in her accomplishment, watching the printer spit out the pages, the door to her office flew open. She jerked around to find Marly standing in the doorway, hands on her hips and face beet red.

"What did you do?" Marly screeched.

"Huh?" Veronica asked, grabbing her coffee mug before it toppled off of her desk.

"I just came from the bridal store for my last fitting. Guess what? The gown didn't fit. Do you know why? Because *you* told them to alter it to a size two and not a size twelve!"

Veronica's jaw dropped. What was Marly talking about?

She hadn't talked to anyone about the wedding

gown. The last she knew the bridal store would be delivering the gown to Marly the day before the wedding. She shuffled through the paperwork on her desk, trying to see if somehow she had missed a mention of Marly's gown. How could she miss such a detail?

"Marly, I really don't know what you're talking about. I haven't talked to anyone about your gown."

"I knew something like this would happen. I knew you'd pull some crap to try to ruin my wedding. I mean, really, a size *two*? You always made fun of my weight and now you want me to believe you had nothing to do with having my gown altered to a size two?" Marly gestured to Veronica. "By the way, you aren't exactly a size two anymore yourself, you know, so stop the weight shaming!"

Veronica's eyes narrowed, and she swallowed her sarcastic remarks before they spewed out of her mouth. Marly was right. She had tormented her about her weight when they had worked together. And right now they were probably the same size. And the truth was, she didn't even think Marly was overweight.

"Marly, I *swear* I did not call the bridal store!"

"What's going on in here? I can hear you all the way from my office." TJ stood in the doorway, his eyes darting from Veronica to Marly, a confused look on his face.

"She screwed up my wedding gown, and now it doesn't fit!" Marly yelled, pointing a finger at Veronica.

"I did *not* do anything to your gown." Veronica struggled to keep from yelling. She looked at TJ helplessly.

TJ raised his hands. "Okay, calm down. I don't know the whole story, but I do know we don't handle anything to do with the wedding gown, aside from it being delivered here if the bride is getting married on-site."

Marly crumpled the piece of paper she held and threw it across the room, barely missing Veronica's head. "That's the bridal store. *They* told me that someone from *here* called them with the changes. I do *not* have time for this! I have employees waiting on me at work. You two need to *fix it.*" She stormed out.

"Wow. I guess she really is a bridezilla, huh?" TJ said.

"I totally get why she's so pissed off. I would be too. It's a few days before her wedding, and her gown's been altered to fit a stick figure. There's no way they can now magically make it bigger."

Veronica surprised herself with how much sympathy she felt for Marly. Maybe it was because the situation brought back memories of her prom. She had bought the perfect lavender gown, even practiced poses in it for weeks… and then her date had stood her up. No one ever saw her in that gown, except for her mother, who had laughed at her and told her she looked like a fat grape. Veronica knew how important just the right gown was. If she'd felt that way about a prom gown, imagine how Marly felt about her *wedding* dress.

She picked up the crumpled paper, smoothed it out on her desk, and looked for the address of the bridal store.

"Well, here's the address of the bridal store," Veronica sighed. "I just have no idea how to fix the problem. We may have to fork over a lot of money to get a new dress on short notice."

"Maybe I can help," TJ said with his usual optimism.

"You? How could you help? Unless you're also a seamstress in addition to being a dishwasher and a financial wizard."

"Ha ha. Funny. I'm pretty good at talking people into helping me, and I suspect that maybe that's not one of your talents." TJ leaned one shoulder against the doorframe, crossed his arms over his broad chest, and raised an eyebrow. "We might as well go to the store together. We both want Gertie to succeed, right? And besides, I'm just sitting around killing time waiting for your proposal."

Veronica grabbed the papers from her printer and waved them at him. "Well, the good news is the proposal is done. The bad news is this wedding gown fiasco could ruin all of the work I just did."

8

Veronica and TJ took a cab across town to LaScaldena's, a posh boutique that specialized in designer wedding gowns. As they approached the front door, Veronica noted the intercom located beside it, along with the "By Appointment Only" sign.

"Well, this is great. Now what?" Things were already off to a bad start.

TJ just smiled and reached for the buzzer.

A women's voice boomed over the intercom almost immediately. "Yes?"

"Good morning. My associate and I were sent here by one of our clients, Marly West, to discuss her gown. We are from O'Rourke Signature Events." TJ winked at Veronica.

Impressive. Why hadn't she thought of throwing

out the names? Marly and Gertie were fairly well-known in the city.

A buzzer went off, then the door clicked and a petite woman opened it for them, ushering them inside. "Wait here, please. Miss LaScaldena will be with you in a moment."

The boutique consisted of a giant room with glistening black-and-white marble floors and a huge pink crystal chandelier hanging in the middle. Wedding gowns loaded with lace, pearls, and rhinestones sparkled on mannequins and hung from racks. Mahogany-doored dressing rooms dotted the perimeter. Walking by one, Veronica peeked inside and saw the dressing room was actually more like a suite, with a room covered in mirrors and a platform in the middle for the bride to stand on. Champagne glasses, too? She really could use a drink right about now.

"How may I help you?" A monotone voice interrupted Veronica's gawking, and she looked over to see a tall, older woman who looked as if she were dressed for a funeral staring at her and TJ. Her ankle-length black dress was paired with a pearl necklace and earrings. Her lips were perfectly applied with vibrant pink lipstick. Veronica couldn't help but stare at them. She wondered if they glowed in the dark. Maybe it was a new wedding trend or something.

"Hello. I'm Veronica St. James, and this is TJ... er..."

TJ held out his hand to the woman. "TJ Flannery. Nice to meet you."

Veronica felt like an idiot, she couldn't even introduce TJ because she didn't remember his last name! Ugh! Pull yourself together; don't be such an amateur, she told herself, resisting the urge to slap on more lip balm.

"Our client, Marly West, was here earlier, and there seems to be some kind of a mix-up with her gown," Veronica explained, noticing the woman's jaw tighten as soon as she said Marly's name.

"Yes, yes, Marly. Of course. I'm Viviane LaScaldena. I worked with Ms. West personally on creating her gown. A beautiful gown, really. She has a great eye for design. It is truly a stunning gown. Unfortunately, when she was in early this morning, the gown didn't fit well. It's a shame, really."

Veronica and TJ looked at each other, surprised at the woman's calm.

"So you're aware you made the dress too small? I mean, you didn't make it to Marly's size," TJ said matter-of-factly.

"No, no. I'm sure we made it according to what we were told. We simply would not make a mistake like that. Ms. West must have gained weight. Let me look at her file." The woman walked to an elegant, mirrored 1930s-style desk and picked up a card. "Yes, see? Right here."

The woman turned the card toward them, and they both squinted to make sense of the scribbling.

"Where did you say you were from? O'Rourke's? Someone called in the new measurements from there yesterday morning. It's all right here in the notes. Look." Viviane tapped the card with a perfectly polished nail. "We worked all night to alter the gown. This is what I told Ms. West when she came in earlier for the final fitting. She was not pleased."

"This makes no sense. You've met Marly. Why would you think she wanted her gown taken in so much? Why didn't you check with her before you made the alterations?" Veronica asked, noting that there wasn't even a name associated with the changes on the card. "Did you at least get the name of the person who asked that the changes be made? I mean, why wouldn't you do that?"

Viviane snatched the card back and squinted at it. She picked up a folder from the desk and flipped through a few pages, pursing her pink lips as she did so.

Finally she glanced up at Veronica, her lips set in a thin line. "*Ms.* St John, I run a very tight ship here. Our wedding gowns are all custom-made, one-of-a-kind creations. Perhaps we didn't get the name of the person who called in these changes, but that doesn't really concern me as only someone with intimate details about the bride would know to call here in the first place."

The woman had a point. Who would have known that Marly's dress was being made here? There could have been many people. Anyone in the wedding party, for example. And anyone that Marly had told. But the person had said they were from O'Rourke's, and Marly had only hired the firm yesterday.

"Regarding why we didn't check with Ms. West prior to making the changes," Viviane continued, "as her wedding planner, I am sure you are aware that she is quite busy designing a new clothing line and receiving calls every day about her wedding gown would be a bit ridiculous. In fact, it is *your* job as her planner to ensure this is all done with minimal interference and stress to her. After all, it's her special day!"

Veronica watched the woman's bright pink lips flapping as she spoke and wondered how all that lipstick didn't smudge all over her face and teeth. So far, this conversation was getting them nowhere closer to having a gown that actually fit Marly. All that had happened was a blame game. As she was deciding on what to say, TJ spoke up.

"Look, we can go back and forth all day about who

is responsible for this. The bottom line is Marly has no gown to wear, and we need to fix that. So what is the next step to get that done?" TJ asked.

Good thing TJ had spoken up. Her response to Viviane wouldn't have been as polite, and probably wouldn't have been very productive.

"Well, her gown needs to be made again. I need all new material. It's about a six-week process. I think I can salvage the crystals. They are hand sewn. But if I can't, that will add another four weeks to the process." Viviane sounded almost bored.

Veronica's heart sank. "What? No! We don't have that much time. We have *seven days*. That's it. We need the same exact gown, in a size twelve, in seven days. No exceptions."

"I'm afraid that is quite impossible." Viviane glanced at the door as if she hoped her assistant would arrive to usher them out.

"But there must be some way," TJ said with his usual calm demeanor and charming smile. Veronica didn't think that would work on this woman. She knew something that might, though. The same thing that usually motivated people to do the impossible—a veiled threat.

"I'm sure you realize this wedding will be in all the local papers and tabloids. You don't want any negative publicity if the gown isn't ready. So how do we make this happen?" Veronica locked eyes with Viviane and refused to look away. She knew when she said "negative publicity" she had grabbed the woman's attention. She would get Marly her gown, no matter what. She refused to fail.

Viviane narrowed her eyes at Veronica. She walked over to another desk, then opened a large book that looked like some kind of schedule. She picked up the pink princess phone on the desk, dialed, and spoke quietly into it for a few seconds before turning to Veronica and TJ with a sour look on her face. "I can have the gown made again in the correct size within your deadline for an extra five thousand dollars."

"*What?*" Both TJ and Veronica yelled.

Viviane rolled her eyes. "This is a custom gown, you realize that? *Custom.* It has hand-sewn crystals on it! And I'm not sure I can salvage much of the original material from the gown as I cut it during the final alteration. And I will have to pay a lot of overtime to my seamstresses. What is important to me is that Ms. West is happy with her decision to work with me to have designed the gown in the first place. I mean, if she should ever want to start a wedding gown line..."

Veronica opened her mouth and then shut it. Okay, so this would mean they would eat an additional five thousand dollars, but Marly would have her gown in time. "Okay, fine. Do it. But let's be clear: no one can make any alteration decisions unless it is Marly or myself. I'll follow up with you in a few days to check your progress. Send the invoice for the five thousand dollars to us."

"As you wish," Viviane nodded her dismissal, and Veronica twirled around and headed out of the store, TJ hot on her heels.

"Are you crazy? Five thousand dollars? This is our first event, and we need to stay in budget," TJ said, hailing a cab.

"Marly needs a dress. And not just any dress. She designed this one herself. We don't have a choice," Veronica said. "I could tell Viviane wasn't going to accept the blame, so I figured we'd just have to pay for it."

"I suppose you're right. But how do you think this happened in the first place? I mean, it's a massive screwup." A cab pulled to the curb, and TJ opened the door for her.

Veronica plopped down in the back of the cab. She was already exhausted, and it wasn't even lunch yet. "Good question. I guess it could have been just a fluke miscommunication."

"Good thinking in there about the publicity. If you hadn't said that, she might not have agreed to make another gown so quickly." TJ squeezed her hand as he sat next to her and then quickly dropped it and told the cab driver where to take them.

Veronica froze, unsure what to think about the hand squeeze. Did it mean something? No, he was probably just happy she'd talked Viviane into making the dress and had probably meant it as an added "good job" gesture. She was sure it signified nothing, because guys weren't into her like that... certainly not guys as good-looking as TJ.

9

Back at the office, Veronica grabbed a cup of coffee and a pack of Peppermint Patties and got to work on the proposal. Now that she had an extra five thousand dollars to shave off, things were becoming difficult at best. She had worked so hard on the numbers and had finally gotten them where TJ needed them to be before this stupid wedding gown disaster.

Lucky thing TJ had gone with her to the bridal shop. His calm demeanor really had helped. But *why* had he gone? He'd seemed worried about making sure things went smoothly for this event for Gertie's sake. Maybe he didn't trust Veronica to fix the problem on her own.

And the hand squeeze? Just co-worker stuff. Yep,

co-workers probably did that all the time, right? Veronica wouldn't know. She'd never had any that she'd gotten along with before now. She slipped her hand into her drawer and grabbed the lip balm, smoothing it on her lips and returning her focus to the budget.

The budget was lean to begin with, and Veronica had already been planning to see if she could use any of the linens Gertie had in storage. Maybe Gertie had other things she could use. Centerpieces, candle holders, chair covers. So many little touches were needed to make the room look just right. If Gertie had some of this stuff from the catering businesses she'd bought out, Veronica would be able to shave quite a bit off the bottom line.

She headed to the elevator. Hopefully Gertie hadn't filled the storage area with a bunch of useless junk. She swiped the lip balm on her lips as the elevator hummed down to the basement. If she didn't find anything good down here, she'd have to do something drastic. Maybe cut out more of the appetizers… or get rid of those little boxes for the extra pieces of wedding cake.

The elevator doors opened, and Veronica squinted into the dimness as a whoosh of damp mildewed air hit her. She hadn't realized how creepy it would be down here.

She exited uncertainly. Maybe she should come back down later. Preferably with someone else. But she didn't have time to waste. She needed to get this proposal done, and besides, it was the middle of the work day. Didn't Gertie have people working down here? It's not as though one of them would be a serial killer or something.

In front of her was a handwritten sign that read "Storage" with an arrow toward a thick wooden door. She pushed it, and the rusted iron hinges creaked, reminding her of every scary movie she'd ever seen. Her heart fluttered, and she swiped more lip balm on her lips.

The storage area was massive, running almost the entire length of the mill. There were shelves everywhere. Old tables. Dress forms. Clothing racks. Had Gertie bought out every store that had ever gone out of business?

The space was broken up by several rooms that ran along the outer walls. Veronica glanced at the items on the shelves, but there was so much stuff, she couldn't hone in on anything in particular. Hopefully the linens wouldn't smell moldy or she'd have to have them dry-cleaned, and that would add yet another cost.

She started to poke through the items, hoping to find some candles or linens, but her search was quickly interrupted when she heard voices approaching. She froze and listened. Shoot, it was Marly and her best friend, Sarah Thomas!

If Marly saw her poking through this old stuff, she might kick up a fuss. And Veronica wasn't too keen on seeing Marly after the wedding dress fiasco.

Why were they even here? Gertie must be showing them around or something. Veronica quickly ran to one of the rooms, opened the door, and ducked inside. She stood still for a minute, listening for the voices when...

Slam!

The heavy door slammed shut! She let out a yelp, then covered her mouth with her hands and stood completely still for a minute, her eyes adjusting to the darkness. She fumbled for the door handle, finally located it, and turned it to no avail. She tried again, twisting the handle repeatedly.

It was no use; she was locked in.

HARPER HURRIED out through the thick wooden door before crossing to the large open area near the windows that she'd set up for Marly and her maid of honor, Sarah.

She was certain they wouldn't hear Veronica through the door all the way on the other side of the basement. She felt a slight pang of guilt at shutting Veronica in the room with the faulty doorknob, but she wouldn't leave her in there forever. Just long enough to get Marly riled up and hopefully cause more problems for both of them.

She greeted the two women, careful not to mention her name so they couldn't report her later. Harper tried not to laugh at the horrified looks on their faces as they surveyed the items she'd laid out on the table. She'd chosen some pretty hideous things. Table linens that looked like they were from the dark ages and a bunch of brass monkeys that she assumed had once been centerpieces. They had a hole in the middle for flowers and were absolutely horrid.

"What is this crap?" Marly asked as she and Sarah stood in front of the layout of old linens and hideous brass centerpieces, picking one of the gaudy centerpieces up and waving it in front of Sarah with a confused look on her face. "Is this a monkey?"

"Whatever it is, it's ugly!" Sarah replied, making a face.

"Well, these are a few of the things that your wedding planner said she was planning to use," Harper explained, a smile planted on her face.

"What? No way!" Marly and Sarah both exclaimed in unison. Marly dropped the monkey centerpiece, and it thudded loudly as it landed on the table.

"You're kidding, right?" Sarah asked.

Harper shook her head.

"I'm not using this in the wedding. The linens look like leftovers from a wedding that took place in 1970. And the centerpieces are absolutely hideous. I mean, they're monkeys for crying out loud!" Marly shot a disgusted look at the items laid out on the table. "This is not at all what I want at my reception! Is this some kind of joke? Are we on camera?"

"No, it's not a joke. I'm really sorry. I don't know anything about the selection process. I was asked to get all of your stuff together so you could see it." Harper tried to look apologetic, but she was secretly thrilled at Marly's reaction. She had picked the worst of the items that were being donated to local homeless shelters or thrown in the trash.

"I can't believe she did this. I knew this would happen! It's like she's doing the opposite of what a real wedding planner would do!" Marly paced the length of the table, agitated. "Like I have time to deal with this crap. She's incompetent. Maybe I should just work from here because I seem to have to be here every day anyway. What a waste of a trip."

"I don't even know what to say. I am so sorry, really!" Harper exclaimed, sounding as sincere as she could.

"It's not your fault." Marly managed a tight smile,

giving Harper second thoughts about what she'd just done. She actually seemed kind of nice. But Harper knew she wasn't. At least not according to Uncle Tanner.

Marly stormed off to the elevator with Sarah behind her, both of them talking about how incompetent and stupid Veronica was.

Harper listened to them until they were on the elevator, yet again feeling a slight pang of guilt. Messing around with someone's wedding was bad. Marly had been really upset. But if Veronica was her friend, why had she and Sarah said such mean things about her? If they really were friends, they all seemed like backstabbers, just as Uncle Tanner had said they were.

VERONICA FUMBLED around the dark room for what seemed hours until she found the light switch on the wall opposite the door. Flipping it, she squinted as the fluorescent lights clicked and hummed softly as they lit the room.

In front of her were shelves full of items she might use for Marly's reception: crisp white linens, candles, a guest book, even some really cute items for place cards for guests.

They all fit the low-key theme that Marly wanted. Simple yet elegant. She started to gather the items on an empty table in the middle of the room before going back to the door, hoping that someone had noticed she was missing by now and was looking for her. She didn't hear anyone outside.

She banged on the door.

"Hello? Anyone out there?" she yelled.

Nothing.

She tried again.

She stared at the door, trying to figure how she could break it down when the knob rattled. Then something heavy smashed against the door. She jumped back just as it flew open and TJ skidded inside.

"Oh, hi. I thought I heard you in here," TJ said, holding onto the door to regain his balance.

"What are *you* doing down here?" Veronica asked.

TJs brows lifted. "What are you doing hiding in this room?"

"I'm not hiding. I got locked in."

TJ bent down to inspect the knob. "Really? It locks from the inside."

"What?" Had she locked herself in by mistake? If so, then why couldn't she open it, but TJ had from the outside? "Then how did you open it?"

TJ rattled the knob. "Looks like it's broken. Must

have gotten jammed when you shut the door. I guess that's why I had to jiggle it and push hard to open. You should really leave the door open when you are in a creepy basement like this. Haven't you ever watched a horror movie?"

"Very funny. I didn't close the door." Had someone pushed it closed after her? No, probably just gravity. These old floors weren't level and... "Wait... you like horror movies?"

"Yep. Used to watch them with my sister all the time." TJ flashed a boyish smile that chased the scary basement feeling away.

"So what *are* you doing here?" Veronica asked.

"Gertie sent me to check out what was going on down here. Apparently Marly had some questions for her that didn't make much sense. She didn't like the stuff you picked out for the reception or something like that." TJ eyeballed the items Veronica had placed on the table. "Then I heard you yelling behind the door. Lucky thing. You could have been in here a while."

"Huh? How could she not like them if she hasn't even seen them yet? I literally *just* picked this stuff out. And I've been locked inside this stupid room the whole time."

TJ shrugged.

"I don't know. I only know she wasn't happy. She blew into Gertie's office like a hurricane."

"Well, who showed her the stuff then?" Veronica asked, becoming agitated. So she *had* heard Marly and Sarah. Someone had brought them down here and shown them the wrong things. Had it been on purpose? And if so, who did it, and more importantly, why?

"I don't know. Look, I'm just the messenger boy here. Gertie was wheeling around looking for you, and I offered to see if you were down here because I couldn't find you anywhere else. We can figure out later who showed her the wrong stuff, but for now, I'm still waiting on that proposal. Edward is antsy about the final figures."

Veronica sighed. TJ was right. Figuring out who had done it would have to wait. The proposal was the priority. Besides, she knew Marly would love the things she had just found.

"Okay. Can you help me carry this stuff upstairs? This is going to knock a few thousand off the proposal. I'll get back on it as soon as we get this upstairs."

"That's a lot of stuff. Let's see if there's a cart or something down here. I think I passed one," TJ said as he headed out to the main room, Veronica right behind him.

Several carts were parked in the corner. As Veronica walked over to grab one, she spotted the table of crappy linens and monkey centerpieces.

"Wait. What's this crap?" she asked, running her fingers along the coarse linens and sticking her finger through one of the many holes, holding it up for TJ to see.

"I don't know, but look at these things. What the heck are they? Besides ugly, I mean." TJ held up one of the monkey centerpieces.

Veronica gasped. "Wait. Is this the crap that Marly thinks is for her reception? I would have stormed into Gertie's office like a tornado too!"

"No kidding. If it is, someone is playing a very mean joke." TJ shook his head at the table and then pushed the cart back toward the room where Veronica had piled the real items for Marly's reception.

Veronica followed, pausing to look back at the table full of hideous crap. A joke? She didn't think so. It seemed as if someone was trying to ruin Marly's wedding and in the process, get her fired. The question was who, and why?

10

"Hm. Let's see. No shrimp cocktail at the reception. That knocks off a couple thousand, but I seriously doubt Edward would be happy without it. So maybe just cut it in half and use regular shrimp instead of jumbo shrimp." Veronica talked out loud to herself as she reworked the wedding budget.

She'd been able to reduce the costs fairly well, thanks to all the material she'd found in storage, but that extra wedding gown expense had really messed things up. She just needed to get a bit more creative to slash some more money. She was so close!

"We have a bit of a problem!" Gertie's voice rang through the air as she wheeled herself into Veronica's office. "Marly went bridezilla again, something about tacky brass monkey centerpieces and tattered table linens? What the heck did you show her that junk for?"

Gertie had rolled her wheelchair next to the plant in the corner of Veronica's office and ran one of the dying leaves between her fingers.

"Huh? I haven't even shown her anything yet." Veronica grabbed the watering can she had found downstairs and emptied it into the semilifeless plant. She had meant to water it yesterday, had even filled the watering can on one of her coffee runs to the break room, but had forgotten to actually water the plant.

"Well, someone showed her some of the crap that's been tagged to donate to the shelter. I assumed it was you. Everything that's in bay three is for the homeless, not our customers. Now she thinks you planned to use that junk at her reception!" Gertie was obviously agitated.

Veronica sat down in one of the cushy club chairs next to Gertie's wheelchair.

"It wasn't me. I got locked in one of the storage rooms earlier today. While I was locked in, I found some great stuff for the wedding. Table linens and place cards, some dishes and chargers. All elegant yet simple, as well as saving us money because we don't have to rent or buy any now. But I don't know who would have shown Marly the wrong things. Whoever it was could be the person who locked me in."

"Locked you in? What is this, a regular Nancy Drew mystery with wrong wedding gowns, crappy centerpieces, and people getting locked in rooms?" Gertie snickered.

Veronica reached for one of the sticks of lip balm on her desk. Gertie had a point. Maybe she was over-reacting. "Okay, maybe that was an accident, and if all that stuff was out on a table, maybe Marly saw it and just assumed that was for her reception?"

Gertie wheeled her chair around so she faced Veronica. "This wedding must go off without a hitch. It simply must be perfect. It is our first event, and Marly and Jasper are well-known in this city. I've always trusted my instinct, and my instinct told me to hire you to run my events. Did I make the wrong choice?"

Veronica's eyes burned. Oh no, not now! She wasn't going to cry. She needed to act professional! She pinched the skin between her thumb and fore-finger to stop the flood of tears. She'd learned the old trick in middle school when the kids all made fun of her.

"Gertie, you made the right decision. I promise.

This wedding reception will be amazing and the talk of the town. Everything is on schedule, and Marly will be thrilled with the results."

Gertie eyed Veronica skeptically and then nodded quickly before wheeling herself out of the office without a word, making Veronica even more anxious.

She sat back behind the desk to finish the proposal, swiping on more lip balm and nibbling her lip a bit. The waxy cherry-flavored balm soothed her. She hacked away at the budget, cutting out the champagne fountain and replacing it with a champagne toast. Edward might balk, but they had an open bar, and Veronica was sure Gertie could persuade him that they could stock the bar with plenty of champagne if need be. She whittled away at some of the food and finally finished up.

Just as she was hitting the print key on her computer, a knock on the door gave her a jolt. She turned in her chair to see TJ with a worried look on his face.

"Sorry if I startled you. Any progress on the budget?" he asked as he took a seat across from her.

"Just finishing it up now. I'm printing a copy and emailing it to you as well." Veronica's printer whirred to life and started to spit out the budget. TJ grabbed the papers, nodding his head slowly as he looked the pages over.

"Nice. This looks good. Under budget; that's pretty impressive." He winked at her as he thumbed through the proposal, and Veronica felt a surge of pride bubble up—along with another strange feeling as his eyes lingered on hers.

It may have taken what seemed like forever, but she had done it. The proposal had come in under budget and on time.

"It's been a long day. I don't know about you, but I could use a drink. I was going to grab one at O'Brien's down the street. Care to join?" TJ asked casually.

Veronica's heart rolled in her chest. Is that what co-workers did after work or did he mean something else by the invitation? Her hand tingled where he'd squeezed it. Ugh. She was being silly, of course. It was just a co-worker thing. If nothing else, she liked TJ's incessant optimism. It might be fun to get to know him better and maybe even have him for a friend.

"Sounds great," Veronica said, shutting down her computer and reaching for her purse. "I'll meet you out front. I just want to run to the ladies' room first."

Inside the ladies' room, Veronica stared at herself in the mirror. Hair up or down? It was down, but she felt as if maybe she looked better with it up. Wait. If she put it up, TJ might think that was strange. She opted to keep it as it was and ran her fingers through it.

Opening her purse, she grabbed some lipstick, wiped off the greasy lip balm and swiped the lipstick across her lips. She didn't look too bad, passable she supposed, though she doubted TJ would even notice.

11

"All set?" TJ asked as she walked through the reception area toward him.

"Yep. Should we walk there? It's on the next block, right?"

TJ nodded. "We'll probably get there faster that way."

They walked the busy sidewalk and ducked into the bar, which was about a block from the office. Veronica had walked past the Irish pub hundreds of times but had never been inside of it.

TJ held the heavy wooden door for her, and she walked ahead of him into the busy bar. It was dark, a combination of only two windows, the dark woodwork from the floors and bar, and the dimmed lighting. The walls were covered in various pictures of all things Irish, and a giant Irish flag hung on the middle of the side wall. Booths lined the walls. They meandered toward the back, tucking themselves into one of the smaller ones meant for two.

A waitress appeared almost immediately, and Veronica ordered a beer and TJ a soda, making Veronica wonder if she should have ordered something nonalcoholic. She had assumed he would get a beer when he had said he needed a drink.

He leaned back in the booth, looking relaxed and content, and she told herself to just chill out and enjoy his company, and to stop second-guessing everything. He probably didn't order a drink because he'd been out late last night or something, or maybe he was hungover. Besides, this is kind of business-related. It's not as if he had asked her out on a date.

"Cheers," TJ said as he raised his glass.

"Here's to the first proposal being done within budget." Veronica tapped her glass lightly against his.

"So how do you like working for Gertie here? A bit different than on the cooking show, isn't it?" TJ asked as he eyed the menu.

"Yeah, not having the stresses of a daily TV taping is good, but there are other stresses with the tight timeline. Gertie's been great, though. Not a micromanager at all, which is really the only thing that worried me when I took the job. I'm grateful she gave me this opportunity."

"Me too. She believed in me. I doubt I would have landed a good job like this without her. Gotta hand it to Gertie, she seems to like to 'collect' people and give them second chances."

Veronica wondered just exactly why TJ wouldn't have gotten a good opportunity. What was his deal, anyway? Had he done something bad in his past... as bad as the things she had done?

TJ continued, "Between you and me, I know that she's sunk everything she has financially into O'Rourke Signature Events. If this wedding isn't amazing, it could sink her business." TJ's face turned grim, and Veronica saw he really cared about Gertie and her business.

Veronica nodded. Hearing that made her more determined to ensure that Marly's wedding was a success and Gertie's business would be *the* place to host an event. But for once in her life, her determination wasn't just about *her*. She really cared that Gertie was successful.

"The wedding *will* be amazing," she said confidently, locking eyes with him.

"So what did you do before you met Gertie? How did you come to work on the chef show?" TJ asked as he closed the menu and placed it on the table.

"Oh, um, I was an administrative assistant. That's how I know Marly actually. And then for the show, I knew someone who was able to get me a job." Veronica hoped TJ wouldn't press her for more details about her past as she glossed over it. She didn't want him to know about the horrible things she had done and how mean she had been to Marly before. "How about you? You told me a little, but there has to be more."

"Not much more to tell really. I was an accountant and had a run of bad luck. Eventually ended up on the island as a dishwasher. That's the past, though. Like you, I'm grateful things are better now."

Veronica could tell by the way that TJ had glossed over his past that he didn't want to elaborate, and she was fine not pushing him further, even if she was curious. She admired him for pushing through whatever had happened. Being in charge of finances was a good job with a lot of responsibility. He probably wanted to stick to co-worker topics.

"It looks like the weather will hold out for the wedding. There're so many people attending that I'm having the dance floor extended into the tent. So much for ten percent of the people invited not coming! There were only ten people who declined. So about three-hundred people will attend. I know Gertie said that almost all the staff will be working the wedding. Do you think you will go?" Veronica hoped that he would.

"The tent?" TJ asked, his face draining of color.

"Um, yeah. You know, the big white tent?" Veronica wasn't sure if there was an issue with the tent that she wasn't aware of. She reached for her lip balm. "It didn't cost anything, so don't worry. Gertie already had it. You know, huge white tent with sides."

"I know what you're talking about. I'm just not a fan of tents. I was in one once that caught fire, and I could have died. I mean, I almost did die. I just... I don't like being anywhere near them anymore. It freaks me out."

"Oh, I'm so sorry." Veronica studied TJ. So that must be part of his mysterious past. Had he been a firefighter or something? Or maybe it had happened camping? Probably better not to ask. She could tell that TJ was serious, his usually cheerful and upbeat demeanor replaced by nervousness and what seemed to be fear.

The waitress interrupted the awkward moment, and they decided to order potato-skin appetizers. When the waitress left, Veronica decided to change the subject from tents to what was really on her mind.

"So I think someone might be messing with us. I mean, with Marly's wedding. First, there's the wedding gown alterations fiasco. Then I get locked in the storage area, and someone just happens to show Marly the wrong things for her wedding. It's kind of strange, don't you think?"

TJ sipped his drink and thought about it. "Nah. I mean, the dress thing could easily just have been a misunderstanding. And the door in the storage area, well, those doors are all old and heavy. And the floors down there are all uneven. The weight of the door could have easily pulled it shut on you. There're so many people working for Gertie that someone could have shown Marly the wrong things by mistake. I mean, Gertie takes it all on herself, and I can already see people get confused a bit because she has some of them doing the same jobs. She definitely needs a few managers."

"You're probably right. I mean, why would someone want to sabotage Marly's wedding? I should just shut up and focus on making it to the actual wedding day."

TJ laughed. "So, funny coincidence that we end up working together again, huh?"

"Yeah. Will you be washing the dishes at the wedding?" Veronica cringed at her lame attempt at a joke. Hopefully he wouldn't think she was talking down to him.

But he laughed. "I hope not. But I will if I have to. Whatever it takes." He tilted his glass toward her.

"Agreed. Whatever it takes." Their eyes met as she clinked her glass against his, and for a split second she thought maybe they were toasting more than just pulling off the wedding. Maybe a long fruitful association working together. Maybe even a friendship.

The waitress brought their order, and they focused on putting the bubbling cheese-topped potato skins on their plates. Veronica was careful to take only a small amount. She didn't want to blow her diet.

"So what brings you to New York? I mean besides Gertie. Are you from here?" TJ asked as he spooned sour cream on top of the skin.

"Yes. Upper State growing up. I moved to the city after high school. I just wanted to get away." She left out the part about how she had left because her mother had treated her so badly her whole life. And how she had basically lived with no money the first few years, causing her to lose a ton of weight.

"Wow. So you just moved to the city on your own? No job?" TJ asked, seeming genuinely interested.

"Yep. No plan, just a suitcase filled with hope, and some money I had saved for years. I worked some odd jobs and found an apartment with a bunch of other people. It was far from the glamorous city life I had envisioned, but I learned a lot." It was true. Those times had been hard, but Veronica had learned a lot on her own. Plus, anything was better than living with her mother.

"Wow! I totally didn't picture you being that type," TJ said, laughing and signaling the waitress for another round.

"What?! What type?" Veronica asked, having no idea what he meant.

"I mean, I assumed you came from a wealthy family. That's all. Not that there's anything wrong with that. I think it's awesome that you came to the city with nothing. That takes some guts."

Veronica's cheeks burned. Was TJ flirting with her?

"What about you? Did you grow up in the city?" She felt like an idiot echoing his question. Why didn't she ask him something more interesting? She sounded like a parrot, for crying out loud. She grabbed her trusty lip balm and slicked it across her lips as he answered her question.

"I grew up in the Burroughs but interned in the city and moved here in college." TJ took another potato skin and then pushed the plate to her. "Have some more."

Veronica cut off another small piece. The conversation flowed, and Veronica found herself having a great time, relaxing and laughing at the stories TJ told. She opened up to him a bit about the issues she'd faced when growing up, something she usually didn't tell anyone. Soon the lights came on, and the bartender yelled, "Last call."

TJ grabbed the check and laid money down to pay the bill before Veronica could even object. She started to reach for her wallet, insisting that she would at least leave the tip.

"Absolutely not. You can pay next time," TJ said casually as he started to get up.

She slid out of the booth, and they walked outside. The air was cool, and the sky was clear, with the moon shining above the city. The sidewalk was busy with people, the street packed with a mixture of cars and cabs, the usual for New York City.

"Do you live far from here?" TJ asked.

"I live a few blocks that way," Veronica said, pointing to the right. "How about you?"

"I live down there," TJ said, pointing in the opposite direction. "Let me grab a cab for you."

He stepped off the sidewalk and held his arm up to signal for a cab. One pulled up almost immediately, and he opened the door for her, then stood sort of leaning on the cab. She'd have to brush very close to get in.

Veronica froze. This felt awkward. What should she say? Just a goodbye? Thank you for the dinner? It wasn't really dinner, though. It was appetizers. What if he tried to kiss her? She realized she was standing there like a dolt while TJ was holding the door open, so without even thinking she scooted past him into the back of the cab, mumbling "See you tomorrow" as she did so.

The cab door shut, and the driver accelerated, leaving Veronica shaking her head. Real nice. "See you tomorrow." Pull yourself together, Veronica!

TJ WATCHED the cab slowly move through the thick traffic. Veronica had surprised him. She'd changed a lot since their time on the cooking show. She was less bossy. And she looked more put-together. She was smart too. He hadn't picked up on that on the island. Tonight he'd had a glimpse of what went on behind her snarky facade. She wasn't self-centered as he'd thought. She actually cared about Gertie.

He had to admit that with everything going on with the wedding he felt a bond with Veronica. It was up to the two of them to make sure this wedding was successful so that Gertie's business would thrive. And, even though he'd made light of her fears that someone was trying to sabotage the wedding, he had to admit that he had his suspicions about that as well.

Funny, though, that she'd skirted any questions that had to do with her past. Did she have something to hide? Then again, TJ had done the same. He hadn't wanted her to know that he'd been a drug addict. He'd gotten clean and was working his way back, but he still was ashamed of what he had been, and somehow it mattered to him what Veronica might think of him.

TJ turned away and started walking back to his small apartment. No sense in thinking along those lines. Veronica could never be anything but a co-worker. She'd sent that signal loud and clear when she'd shied away from him and hopped into the cab as if fleeing a serial killer.

And who could blame her? Veronica was competent and capable and attractive. What would she want with someone like him? He was damaged goods. Heck, he couldn't even have a conversation about tents without freaking out. Even though his drug days were well behind him, that was still a part of his past he could never escape.

TJ liked his job, and he wanted, more than anything, for O'Rourke Signature Events to succeed. For that, he'd have to keep on good terms with Veronica. It was better for everyone if he kept it all business between him and Miss St. John.

12

Veronica ran the hair straightener through her thick hair one last time, humming as she did so. She wasn't exactly a morning person, but she had slept deeply and awakened extremely calm and refreshed. TJ had put her mind at ease the night before, and now she was more determined than ever to make this wedding a success. Nothing else would go wrong, and Gertie would see that she hadn't made a mistake by placing her in charge of Marly's wedding.

She dressed, checking her reflection in the mirror. She caught herself wondering if TJ would like the outfit, then pushed that thought from her mind. TJ was smart and cute, and even though he hadn't elaborated on his past, she got the feeling that he'd overcome something. Something more than just a crappy childhood, as she had.

Whatever it was, he'd had to turn things around just as she was doing. She admired that, but she also knew there was no way someone like TJ would be interested in her. Though it made her laugh, the *old* Veronica wouldn't have lowered herself to romantic thoughts about a former dishwasher. She really was changing.

She turned from the mirror and grabbed her purse, reminding herself that she wasn't some silly schoolgirl with a crush. She had a job to do.

Just as she grabbed her phone from the charger, it rang, an incoming text from Gertie.

Bridezilla Alert, get to the office pronto!

Dammit! She grabbed her purse in a rush and hurried out the door, not looking forward to whatever fiasco awaited her at the office. She didn't bother to stop at her office. She headed straight to Gertie's instead.

Marly and Sarah sat at the round meeting table, across from Gertie. In the middle of the table sat an oddly shaped piece of plastic. As Veronica got closer, she saw that it looked as if something had melted at the top of it.

"Hi… er, what's going on?" she asked.

Marly stood and gestured toward the plastic thing.

"What's going on?" she asked, her voice rising. "Oh, the usual. My custom-made cake topper's been ruined. It somehow melted. It was dropped off here yesterday afternoon for the cake. But let me guess. You don't know anything about it, right?"

Veronica's mouth opened and closed as she fumbled for words.

"The topper had a curvy, realistic-sized bride. It was custom made, and it was special because Marly was instrumental in the success of the plus-size line at Draconia. You know, the line that you could wear these days?" Sarah eyed Veronica up and down as she sneered.

Veronica could hardly blame Sarah for being suspicious. Before she'd changed, she'd tried to ruin things for Sarah on the cooking-contest show. Even though Veronica had changed, no one could tell just from looking at her. She would have to *prove* to people that she was no longer the mean person she used to be.

Glancing back at the cake topper, she had a sinking feeling. She'd been ready to believe TJ's optimistic assessment that all the things going wrong were coincidence, but this was one thing too many. Someone was out to ruin the wedding, and she needed to stop that person. But first, she needed to smooth things over and fix this latest problem.

Veronica took a deep breath and focused on

speaking in a calm, even tone. "I'm so sorry. I have no idea how this happened. I didn't even know about the cake topper being here. And as far as the other issues go, the wedding dress is all set. The linens and center-pieces that you were shown weren't the right ones. I apologize for the poor communication."

"Bullshit! I called this from day one. I knew you'd try to mess with my wedding!" Marly yelled as Sarah nodded in agreement next to her.

Veronica struggled to maintain her composure. The older Veronica wanted to bubble to the surface and tell Marly off, but she couldn't do that. One glance at Gertie sent the old Veronica back deep inside. She couldn't ruin things for the old woman.

"Marly, I haven't screwed with anything, I swear! I wouldn't jeopardize O'Rourke Signature Events or my position here."

"Oh *shut up*, Veronica!" Sarah chimed in, rolling her eyes.

Marly stomped over to Veronica, getting in her face. "Yeah, *shut it!* I'm sick of you and this wedding! I'm going to—"

"That's *IT!*" Gertie interrupted, smacking a long stick down on the table, making everyone jump. She typically used the stick to help her grab things from shelves, but she employed it now to stop their argument. "You are all acting like children, and I won't have it!"

"Gertie, I don't care what she says, this was no accident," Marly said quietly as she stared at Veronica. "If it wasn't so close to the wedding date, I would *not* have my wedding here!"

"Dear, calm down. If you think I won't get to the bottom of this, you are wrong. The topper was delivered last night after Veronica left for the day. I hadn't even told her about it yet. For all we know, someone left the topper too close to the stove in the kitchen by mistake." Gertie pressed her lips together and closed her eyes. "Let me remember... I left it in the kitchen. Someone might have moved it. I know it was near six o'clock because I was on my way out for my volunteer work at the hospital. When I came in this morning, I saw it and called you right away. Veronica wasn't even in yet."

Marly looked skeptical. She glanced at Veronica and then Gertie. "Well, who *did* know about it then?" Marly demanded.

"Well dear, I didn't announce that it was here. And what happened would have had to happen between six and seven last night. I locked the doors on my way out, and most of the crew was with me. Security cameras kick on at seven inside the kitchen area, and I already had Logan review them. No one was in the kitchen.

The only way in after-hours is a key card or using the emergency code. No one used their key card."

"Did anyone use the code? How many people know it?" Sarah asked, looking directly at Veronica.

Gertie cast a quick glance at Veronica.

"Well, the head chef has one, and finance, and the event manager…"

Marly planted her fists on her hips and jerked her head toward Veronica. "So *she* has one?"

"Yes," Gertie replied, shifting in her seat.

"Well, this isn't exactly a surprise now, is it? How hard would it be for her to double back, sneak in and—"

Marly's tirade was interrupted by TJ, who had apparently been listening to them from the doorway.

"Veronica couldn't have done it. She was with me last night between six and seven," TJ said, nonchalantly taking a sip of his coffee.

Veronica's heart soared. No one had ever stuck up for her before. But the look of shock on Marly and Sarah's faces threw her. Why would they look so shocked at the fact that she and TJ had gone out together after work? Did they think she was that repulsive that no one would hang out with her?

Gertie smiled, approval in her eyes as they moved from TJ to Veronica. "Well, that settles that. But I don't like this. Who the hell would do such a thing? All these things? I don't like this crap affecting my business."

They all sat silently for a moment before Veronica spoke up.

"Well, I know someone who would like to see us fail. Marly and me, I mean. He's pretty ruthless and will stop at nothing for revenge." Veronica glanced out of the corner of her eye at Marly. "Tanner Durcotte."

Marly's eyes narrowed. "Yeah, right. Last time I looked, you were in cahoots with him."

Veronica shuffled her feet. "I *was*. I admit that. But I'm not like that anymore." She glanced at Sarah. "I'm on his bad side now because I balked at ruining the chef contest for you."

Sarah's mouth tightened. "Really? I just figured you messed up and things didn't work out the way you planned."

"Enough with the bickering," Gertie cut in impatiently. "Who the hell is Tanner Durcotte?"

Marly sighed. "He was a friend of my mother, and when she got sick… well… he made me an offer and then screwed me over."

"He used to own a fashion design company," Veronica said. "He was in competition with Draconia, and he's ruthless."

"Except now his company is out of business, thanks to Marly, and he owns a bunch of restaurants,"

Sarah said. "That's why he wanted to ruin the cooking contest for me. My partner is his biggest competitor."

Gertie nodded. "I see. I know the type. Give me everything you have on this Tanner Durcotte, Veronica. I might need to pay him a visit. I will not have him, or anyone, destroying my new gig or Marly's wedding. And now I need to get to a meeting. You people carry on and figure out what to do to keep things running smoothly with this wedding." Gertie wheeled herself out of the room, TJ practically jumping out of her way she moved so fast.

TJ came into the room, and they all sat at the table, Marly and Sarah casting uneasy glances at Veronica. Clearly they still didn't trust her. Fine. She'd earn their trust one way or the other.

"What's up with this Tanner guy? Why would he want to ruin the wedding? And how would he get access to ruin the cake topper." TJ pointed to the melted thing in the middle of the table.

"It's kind of a long story." Veronica did not want to explain all the details about Tanner. "Tanner wouldn't do this himself. He'd have somebody doing it for him. An accomplice." Guilt pinched her gut.

"Yeah, usually *you're* the accomplice," Sarah said as she rolled her eyes.

"Really, Sarah? I thought it was Marly that was the accomplice. Didn't she team up with him at Draconia?" Veronica couldn't stop herself. The truth was that Marly was just as guilty as she was when it came to working with Tanner, so who were they to judge her?

"I had no choice! I did it to save my mother's life!" Marly cried out.

"What's your excuse?" Sarah asked Veronica. "You tried to discredit Marly and ruin the chef contest out of spite!"

"No. Marly was acting against Draconia, and I simply exposed that. I admit I made some bad choices, but I didn't actually end up ruining the contest. Tanner told me to, but I didn't end up doing it! That's probably why he's after me too." Veronica looked down at the table, embarrassed and certain that TJ wouldn't want anything to do with her after this. Oh well, it had felt good to have him stick up for her this one time.

"Okay, I've heard enough," TJ said, rising. "I don't know what's going on between the three of you, but I do know a few things. One is that Veronica wouldn't have done any of the things you think she did to ruin the wedding. She loves this job. She's proud of it and wouldn't risk ruining an event and potentially ruining Gertie's new business."

Veronica squirmed in her chair. "Thank you."

"And I also know that Marly wouldn't want her

wedding messed up. So it must be someone else. So, instead of arguing, how about everyone focuses on the wedding and who might actually be trying to ruin it?"

The three women silently stared down at the table. Veronica thought about all the mean things she'd done to Marly, from name-calling to weight-shaming to trying to get her fired. She regretted it all. But Marly wasn't completely blameless. She had done some bad things, even if for a good reason. Did Marly have regrets too? She hoped so. It was time to move on, as TJ had said.

"Okay, but who else would have access to the building after-hours? And who would call in the dress size change?" Marly asked.

"I don't know, but considering how Veronica fought to have your dress remade instead of just having you get one off the rack, I can tell you she didn't do it," TJ replied, looking at Veronica. "I have an idea how we can find out who it is. But it means you all have to work together. Can you do that?"

Marly and Sarah exchanged glances while Veronica looked at TJ, trying to figure out his plan.

"I don't know. I mean..." Marly started.

"Veronica, I know you have a ton left to do for the wedding. Why don't you go ahead and get to work," TJ said, motioning to the door.

Veronica stood up and left the room in silence. She

was unsure what exactly TJ had in mind, but she was thankful to be out of the room. She had much left to do to pull off the wedding and needed to start her day as soon as possible. As she walked toward her office, the uneasy feeling in her gut tightened. Weird that TJ had asked her to leave the room. He didn't even know Marly and Sarah. What did he plan to tell them that he didn't want her to hear?

13

TJ knew he'd be able to accomplish more if he could persuade Marly and Sarah to trust Veronica, but that wasn't going to happen with Veronica in the room.

He knew Sarah pretty well. She was his sister after all, and even though she was still a little steamed at him for changing his last name and breaking contact when he was in trouble, he knew he could reason with her. He'd had good practice since they'd reconnected, especially when they'd discovered they'd both been associated with the cooking show, even though neither of them had known the other was there.

Sarah had been too busy competing on the show to pay any attention to the kitchen staff, and TJ had focused on not being noticed in the back. He hadn't even paid attention to the chefs in the front kitchen. They had no reason to cross paths. It had taken quite a bit of persuasion to get her to believe he'd had no idea she was there.

"Okay, I have no idea what the drama is between you guys and Veronica, but hear me out. I'm confident that she isn't trying to sabotage the wedding." TJ glanced from Sarah to Marly.

"You don't know how devious she can be," Marly said. "Do you think it's a coincidence she shows up here working with you?"

TJ frowned. "What do you mean?"

"She has it out for Sarah too, and you're Sarah's brother."

TJ wondered about that. He'd never mentioned he knew Marly or Sarah. It never occurred to him because he didn't know Marly that well. He'd seen no indication from Veronica that she knew he was related to Sarah. "How would she know that? I don't have the same last name, and besides, I know how she ended up here. Same way I did: Gertie."

Sarah scowled, but Marly's face softened. "Gertie does have a soft spot for people who might have chosen the wrong path. And she's a good judge of character. She's been wonderful to my mother." She touched Sarah's arm. "Maybe we should listen to TJ. I mean, I did some mean things myself. Maybe Veronica had a reason."

TJ nodded. "Maybe she did some stupid things before, but that's in the past. She's totally committed to kicking ass in this job. She spent hours on the proposal. You need to give her a break. People *do* change. Look at me. What if Gertie hadn't given me this job because she didn't believe I'd changed and would go back to being a drug addict?"

Sarah sighed. "I guess you're right. At least about people making stupid mistakes. I lied to get into the chef contest. I mean, sure, I did it for a good reason, which was to send you to rehab. But it was still a lie. And Marly, you did the same. I mean, it was to save your mom, but it was still a lie."

Marly nodded silently as she stared down at the table. Sarah looked at TJ and shrugged.

"Well, maybe there's a reason Veronica did what she did in the past too," TJ said, sensing that there was. "I really think you guys should let bygones be bygones and work with her. That's the only way we're going to be able to make sure whoever is trying to ruin things doesn't succeed. Please."

The room was quiet for several minutes.

"Fine." Sarah and Marly both said in unison.

"Great! So, now that that's settled, I have a plan to flush out this mole we seem to have."

VERONICA SHOVED the Peppermint Patty she'd grabbed from the break room into her drawer. For some reason, she wasn't hungry. Everything was at stake with this wedding. Her job. Gertie's business.

She was in a mild state of panic over the fact that TJ was now alone with Marly and Sarah. Who knew what they were telling him about her? She had been so happy when he had defended her, but what if Marly and Sarah convinced him otherwise, making her out to be a terrible person?

And why was he alone with them? It seemed weird that the finance guy would want to meet with them alone. Then again, he had as much at stake with this wedding as she did, and it was pretty obvious Veronica, Marly, and Sarah weren't going to agree on anything. Yet, she'd gotten the vague impression that he knew them as more than just Gertie's finance guy, but how?

She pulled out her lip balm and smoothed it on her lips. There wasn't much that she could do about what TJ thought of her, so there was no use dwelling on it.

Besides, she needed to get Gertie the information on Tanner that she had asked for earlier. She'd already gathered some basic material on him and was writing down the names of his restaurants as Gertie wheeled in.

"Hey kid, don't worry about bridezilla and her sidekick," Gertie said. "And we'll figure out who is behind all these strange happenings and show them it's not you."

"Thanks." Veronica's heart warmed at Gertie's faith in her. She handed Gertie the paper. "I wrote down the restaurants that Tanner Durcotte owns."

"Humph. This one is right down the street. What a coincidence. I'm hungry." With that she wheeled herself out of Veronica's office.

14

Gertie hung up her phone and wrote a note to remind her to send flowers to her friend. She had contacts all over the city, and this person had been able to tell her exactly which of his restaurant's Tanner Durcotte would be at for lunch today.

She smoothed her long grey hair back, pulling it behind her ears. Reaching into her purse, she pulled out some lipstick and applied it, a warm pink tone that highlighted her full lips. She applied some blush to her cheeks, adding a pop of color. Next she added some mascara onto her bare lashes, her bright green eyes popping against the jet black. She backed up a bit and studied her reflection, happy with the results. She may be in a wheelchair and pushing sixty-five, but she looked damned good!

She had her driver drop her around the corner from Tanner's restaurant and wheeled herself along the sidewalk, something she usually avoided. People could be so rude in the city, and it wasn't uncommon for someone to tell her that she was in the way or that she needed to move faster or slower or to the right or the left. Damned idiots!

She maneuvered her way down to the restaurant as fast as she could without running someone over. She always knew about any new restaurants in the city. This one had opened right before she had left for the cooking contest, and she'd heard very good things about it. The chef had actually been a runner-up in the cooking show she had produced, just barely missing out on making it onto the show.

The inside was impressive. It was bright and airy, the ceilings extremely high, which was rare for this city. A large bar ran down the center of the room with tables and booths scattered throughout the rest of the space. The front and rear had floor-to-ceiling windows offering great views and abundant light. The wood, all mahogany, shined beautifully, as did the black leather used for all of the seating.

She wheeled herself to the hostess stand, a scowl on her face.

"How am I supposed to be able to get over there?" she asked, pointing at a section toward the back of the restaurant. "The tables are all so damn close that someone in a wheelchair could never get through to that area."

The hostess, a young girl who looked no older than twenty-two, fumbled around with menus, stuttering a lame answer. "Well, I... I guess we could move—"

"Was this place ever inspected?" Gertie asked, interrupting her. "I mean, I guess I can call the city to find out. It's easy to get that info these days."

An older man wearing a suit with a shiny tag that said "Maitre'd" walked briskly across the room from the bar area, approaching Gertie.

"Is there a problem?" His eyes flicked from the hostess to Gertie. "What can I help you with today?"

Gertie threw her arms in the air. "I'm asking about how anyone in a wheelchair is expected to get down to that area over there. Or does the owner just not want disabled people eating here? I mean, we *do* eat out on occasion, you know." Gertie spoke loudly, causing nearby patrons to turn and stare.

"Of course we welcome disabled people! Why don't we find you a table, and I will see if the owner is available." He motioned to the hostess for a menu and grabbed it, then walked around behind Gertie and started to push her wheelchair toward a nice table next to a window.

Gertie bit her tongue to keep from laughing out

loud. What a bunch of idiots! She had played them like a piano. The seating was fine. And she had scored a great table!

"I hope this will do?" The man asked, quickly removing the chair and pushing her up to the table. He took her napkin from the table and handed it to her.

"I guess this is okay." Gertie said, sounding terse.

"Excellent. I will see if the owner can come speak to you."

Gertie nodded her head and opened the menu. She wasn't really that hungry, but the menu was impressive and contained varied dishes. This Tanner guy might be a jerk, but he sure seemed to know how to run a restaurant.

TANNER DURCOTTE STOPPED in his tracks as he approached Gertie's table, almost causing a waiter that was behind him to drop a tray of food. He apologized to the waiter and walked slowly toward the table, eying Gertie cautiously.

She looked almost exactly like his late wife. The long grey hair pulled back from her face. Tan complexion. Bright eyes. And, based on what his employees had said, she was apparently feisty as hell, just as his wife had been.

"Good afternoon Mrs. ... er..."

"O'Rourke. And it's Miss. Call me Gertie. Who are you?" Gertie asked as she eyed him critically.

"Miss... er, Gertie, I'm Tanner Durcotte. I own this restaurant, and I understand there was an issue?"

A waiter appeared and placed several appetizers on the table in front of Gertie. Tanner nodded to him. He had arranged for the best appetizers he had to be sent to the table as soon as he had heard that there was an issue.

"I arranged for some of our award-winning appetizers to be sent over. I do hope that's okay?" he asked, hoping it didn't upset her or that she had a food allergy.

She nodded and then motioned for him to sit down across from her. He pulled the chair back and sat, noticing that her ring finger was bare.

"There's not enough room," Gertie said as she reached for a grilled jumbo shrimp. "Between the tables, I mean. Someone like me can't get through."

Tanner was confused, unsure of what she meant by "someone like me." What did she mean? "Someone like you?"

He watched as Gertie pushed herself back a bit from the table and saw that she was in a wheelchair. He hadn't even noticed it when he had seen her from afar; he had been too mesmerized by her face.

"Oh, I'm sorry, I didn't realize…"

"Realize what? That I was on four wheels?" Gertie asked, wheeling herself close to the table and reaching for one of the sauces that had been set out with the food.

"I'll have the issue resolved immediately. We did have the inspectors here, and they ensured us that we were ADA compliant, but I trust your judgment. I hope you'll accept my sincere apology. Of course your meal will be on the house." Tanner felt himself babbling like an idiot. Why was he over-apologizing for this? Besides, he knew that there was enough room between those tables and chairs for a wheelchair to pass. He'd measured them himself. There was the slight chance someone had moved them around without him knowing. He looked at Gertie again. There was something about her he just couldn't put his finger on, and it flustered him.

He stood, and Gertie waved her hand at him. "No, no. Sit down. Please. I can't eat all of this by myself, and I hate to waste food."

"No, that's okay. I really should be…"

"Sit," Gertie said sternly, staring him right in the eyes.

He sat down, not knowing why he was doing so. He had plenty of other things he should be attending to other than having lunch with someone who had caused a ruckus in his restaurant.

"So, how long have you been in business?" Gertie reached for her second shrimp. "And who runs your kitchen? This shrimp is excellent. Fresh. Cooked to perfection."

Tanner gave her the rundown on how he'd started the business with a single restaurant and expanded it to five within the city. Of course he left out the part about the failed fashion design business. They chatted for more than an hour, with Gertie showing genuine interest in the restaurant, just as his wife had. In fact, no one else had really shown this much interest in him since his wife had died. It felt good.

"What does your wife think of this? The long hours, I mean. Or does she work here too?" Gertie asked.

Tanner hesitated. "My wife passed away a few years ago. Cancer. We had no children." He couldn't say anything else, the words wouldn't come out. He still was unable to talk about it without choking up.

Gertie nodded. "It still hurts, doesn't it? Deep wounds take a long time to heal. But you can't heal them by lashing out at others."

Tanner was taken aback. What did she mean by that? His mind raced to his plan to ruin Marly's wedding and how he had tried to rig the show that Sarah had been on. This woman couldn't possibly know about that, though.

As he stared at her, he suddenly realized he knew who she was. Gertie O'Rourke. The old bat who owned the new event venue where Marly was having her wedding. The same place where Tanner had pulled strings to get Harper employed. But Gertie had used an employment agency for that position. Tanner had a contact there, and they owed him a favor. There was no way Gertie could have known he'd planted Harper there for a reason. Harper would never have told her. Maybe she was just a nutjob.

"I'm not lashing out at anyone, at least not these days." Tanner smiled at her, hoping she couldn't see through him.

"Well, maybe you aren't. But if you were, it wouldn't be right. Especially if it were to ruin someone else's special day. I'm sure you know that karma always finds a way to pay people back. What goes around comes around." With that she placed her napkin on her plate and wheeled herself away, leaving a confused Tanner at the table.

His heart gave an uncomfortable lurch. Emily would have said the same thing if she were alive. She, too, would have reminded him about karma. Then again, if all that karma mumbo jumbo was right Emily wouldn't be dead, would she? His thoughts were suddenly interrupted by an incoming text.

Operation Cake Topper is a success. Awaiting further instructions.

15

Veronica's new leather pumps made a soft pattering as she tapped her foot on the floor. Her nerves were at an all-time high over what had been said after she had left Gertie's office. She was going to find out any second, because TJ was standing in her office. She was positive that at any minute he would call her out on all the mean things she'd done to Marly, and that Sarah had told him about her in their meeting. She reached for the lip balm on her desk.

TJ wasn't acting angry, though. He was relaxed, smiling even. Whatever he had talked to Marly and Sarah about, it must have gone well.

"You don't need to worry about Sarah and Marly giving you a hard time anymore," he said.

"Easier said than done. I mean, I still don't trust

them. Or maybe they don't trust me. Not yet, anyway." She paused to take a swig of her coffee. "I figured I can research the people who work here. You know, to see if any of them have a connection to Tanner. It should be easy to research everyone. There aren't that many people working here, right?"

"There's sixty, maybe a few more."

"*Sixty* people? What do they all do? I've only seen a handful of them around."

TJ shrugged. "You know Gertie. She collects lost souls."

"True. That's a lot of people to go through, though. Why are you so positive that it's not Marly? I mean, do you know her or something?" She knew that it wasn't Marly, but she was dying to know more about TJ's connection to her and hoped that he would spill the beans.

Looking up at him, she reeled herself in. He now sat on the edge of her desk, grinning at her in a way that made her heart flutter.

"It's not Marly. I don't know her that well, but it makes absolutely no sense for her to sabotage her own wedding. She has no reason to. It sounds like this Tanner guy might have a reason, though, right? I mean, it sounds like you know how this guy operates from experience."

Veronica squirmed in her chair. She'd known this

would eventually come up. How could she explain to TJ without losing his respect? Then again, did she even deserve his respect?

"Yes, I did something for Tanner. And just like Marly, I had a reason, and—"

TJ held up his hand, cutting her off. "I don't need the details. That's all in the past. It doesn't matter. It's what you do now—in the present—that matters. Let it go."

His soothing voice calmed Veronica. He was right. She needed to focus on what's happening now. "Okay, so how should I start finding out about the employees?"

"We need to get Gertie's approval first. There's no Human Resources Department, and I'm handling all of the payroll and have all of the new-hire paperwork everyone filled out. Everyone signed a release for reference checks, so I guess we could do that. Most of the files would have the information on their past employers. That's probably the best place to start. Maybe we'll find a link to this guy's fashion company or one of his restaurants," TJ said as he slid closer to Veronica and tapped the computer screen.

His arm brushed against hers, and Veronica tried to ignore the spark that flared inside her. Did he feel it too? No, he was studying the computer screen. She thought back to the hand squeeze and the way he'd acted when they'd gone out after work. She had kind of gotten a vibe. Maybe she should suggest going out for a drink again. But before she could, Gertie's squeaking wheels broke the silence.

"I just had a delightful lunch with your friend Tanner. Not a bad guy, really. I think he just needed to hear a few things to set him straight. I don't think he will be bothering us again."

Veronica couldn't believe that someone as savvy as Gertie could be snowed by Tanner. The fact that she had had lunch with him blew her away.

"Gertie, you have no idea how ruthless he is. I don't know what the two of you said to each other, but trust me, he's not giving up. He must have someone doing his dirty work from inside, because he always has someone else do his dirty work. If you approve, I can run a background check on all the employees and see if I can find a connection."

"Absolutely not!" Gertie shot her a stern look. "I will not allow my employees to be checked up on as if they are criminals. Are you off your rocker? That's an invasion of privacy! How would you two like it if I did that to you?"

Veronica glanced at TJ. She wouldn't like that very much at all and judging by the look on his face, neither would he.

"I didn't think so," Gertie said. "Now, I told you

that Tanner won't be pulling any more shenanigans. That's that. Now stop playing detective, and get back to work. We have a wedding to pull off in five days!"

Gertie wheeled out and Veronica turned to TJ. "Well, this isn't good. I know Tanner, and I know if he's out to ruin someone, he won't stop. How the hell are we going to find out who the mole is before they do more damage?"

"Don't worry," TJ said. "I've got a plan."

———

TANNER SAT at the table alone, waving off the approaching waiter. He fidgeted with the flatware, noting a few spots on the butter knife. Don't they know they should be hand-drying the cutlery to avoid spots? He grabbed his phone and entered a reminder in his notes to reprimand the restaurant manager about it at the next meeting. He looked at the empty chair across from him where Gertie had sat and felt a pang of loneliness. He had enjoyed her company and their chat. Maybe she was right, maybe lashing out wasn't the thing to do.

He got up and walked to the rear of the restaurant, past the tables that Gertie had complained about being too close together. He stopped for a minute, then went to the hostess stand for the tape measure. He measured the space between the chairs. Just as he thought; it was fine. Hm. The old bat didn't know what she was talking about.

The closer he got to his office, the more he wondered what had come over him at the table. Sure, Gertie looked like Emily, but so what? She wasn't Emily, and she had no business coming in here and talking about table distances and trying to make him feel guilty for seeking the revenge he deserved. Marly and Veronica had done him wrong, and he just wanted to even the score. Isn't that what karma was all about?

He entered his office and avoided looking at his wife's photo. Instead, he looked at the text from Harper on his phone. Operation Cake Topper had gone off without a hitch. But for some reason the victory tasted sour.

It was no coincidence that Gertie O'Rourke had shown up at his restaurant. Tanner decided to call around and do some checking, see what she was up to. But all he found out was that Gertie had sunk a lot of money into her new venue and had been buying up stock from venues that had gone out of business. Tanner had to admit that was a smart move. A new operation needed to cut costs, and some of the equipment at those places was almost new. Of course it did create a mess to sort through, but that's how he'd been able to place Harper there from the agency he'd used.

"You're sure that's who bought them?" Tanner was talking to an old buddy who used to run a large catering service.

"Yep. O'Rourke Signature Events bought everything we had. Warming trays. Linens. Plates. She got a great deal too. Some of it was crap, though."

"Crap? What do you mean by that?" Tanner had heard O'Rourke Signature Events wanted to establish itself as a top-notch venue. Why would there be a bunch of junk there?

"Well, it was sold in a lot, so she had to buy it all. I wasn't gonna sell it piece by piece. A bunch of the chairs are bad. As soon as someone sits down, the chair will break on them. Oh, and the poles. The tent poles. A bunch of the wooden ones are rotted. Now those should be thrown away immediately. You tell your friend to get rid of the ones with the red tags. They could do some serious damage if they're used!"

Tanner thanked his friend and ended the call. Tent poles. Interesting.

16

They were still working on the ballroom that would host Marly's wedding reception. A few patches of plaster here, some paint there. One man was fixing something on the wall. Gertie had ordered tables set up in the back room, and the linens and napkins were being ironed by hand. No fancy machines here. Gertie wanted everything perfect. She wheeled from room to room, inspecting the work and issuing words of encouragement to her crew.

Even though the room wasn't complete, it looked amazing. Veronica was happy with how it had come along, and even happier that TJ had a plan to figure out who the mole was—and that he trusted her enough to make her part of the plan. Okay, so Marly and Sarah were included too, but still, it felt good to be included. She had never been included in anything growing up or at any of her previous jobs. It was always just her, alone.

She headed to the front desk to meet Marly. Part of TJ's plan was to have a walk-through of the ballroom area and kitchen with Marly in front of the entire staff. They intended to lay a trap for the saboteur.

They walked toward the reception room in awkward silence. Veronica didn't really know what to say or how to say it. Telling Marly she wanted a truce or that she was sorry seemed too dramatic, so she opted for silence.

"Well, here it is," Veronica said as she opened the double doors that led to the giant room. "It's not complete yet, of course. But this should give you a general idea. What do you think?"

Marly stood in silence, and Veronica could tell that she approved. Why wouldn't she? The room was gorgeous. The honey-colored aged oak floor gleamed, flecks of light from the crystal chandelier shimmered on the floor and walls. The walls had gorgeous sconces directing a warm pinkish hue from the top and bottom. Straight ahead was the glass wall, the soft water of the river in plain sight behind it. The wall fountain toward the end of the room bubbled softly, the mesmerizing sound of the trickling water soothing in the hubbub of the room.

"These are the flowers I picked out. Not too fancy. I thought they were simple, but elegant." Veronica pointed to a table that had been set with some of the flowers. There were soft lilac-colored roses and daises intertwined. The colors mixed together beautifully, and the lilac matched the bridesmaids' dresses as well as the decorative bows on the backs of all of the chairs.

"It's all really beautiful, Veronica. I mean, gorgeous. The flowers are perfect."

Veronica's heart swelled with pride. Marly actually sounded sincere, and Veronica realized how important Marly's approval had been to her. Maybe it was the first step in trying to make things right. "I'm so happy you like it. I wasn't sure if I should go with white roses or have them colored, but once I saw the color of your bridesmaids' dresses, I figured color was the way to go. It adds just the right punch of color, and it mixes so well with the yellow in the daisies. Hopefully Edward agrees. I know he wanted a variety of flowers."

Marly rolled her eyes. "Well, you know Edward. He's very critical."

"You can say that again."

Marly laughed, and Veronica felt a tug at her heart. Marly wasn't making fun of her or angry. She was laughing *with* her. It was as if all the bad events of the past had disappeared, and Marly was treating Veronica like a real person for the first time. Of course that might be because Veronica was treating Marly like a real person. Funny, because they were so much alike and even might have been friends if things were different. Maybe there was still time.

"I think even Edward will like these. And I love the room. It's just all pulled together so nicely in such a short amount of time. I really can't believe you pulled this off." Marly leaned closer to Veronica and lowered her voice. "It's even better than my original choice."

She didn't know what had brought about the change in Marly, but Veronica suspected it might have something to do with what TJ had said in Gertie's office the other day. Had Marly truly realized that Veronica had simply made mistakes just as Marly had? In any event, TJ had convinced Marly that Veronica wasn't the one messing with the wedding, and for that, she was grateful. Maybe Marly's newfound friendliness had something to do with feeling a bond at working together on the plan to catch whomever was messing with the plans.

"If anyone told me six months ago I'd be planning your wedding, I'd have called them crazy," Veronica confided, adjusting one of the tablecloths.

"Me too." Marly smiled, then looked out the

window as if she wasn't ready just yet to forgive all. Nor should she be. There was a lot of water under the bridge, and it would take time and effort to make up for what Veronica had done.

"I truly want your wedding to be spectacular," Veronica said.

"Thanks." Marly turned her gaze back to Veronica and glanced at her outfit. "You look good, by the way. I mean, you look better than you did at Draconia. More filled out. There're some great outfits from my line that would look amazing on you."

Veronica was humbled. After all the crap she had given Marly about her weight, here was Marly telling her she looked good.

"I love your line. And thanks for the compliment. To be honest, I feel better at this weight. And I'm so much healthier than when you knew me before. Back then, all I ate were M&Ms."

They laughed together, and Veronica caught a glimpse of what it might be like to have a friend to laugh with. Had she ever had that? Not since she was a child. It felt good, though. Maybe she should work on that.

"Hi, girls." Gertie wheeled herself past them to the dance floor and pointed toward the outside area. "Sorry that the tent isn't up yet, Marly, but you can see it's going to be spectacular out there."

"It's going up in a bit," Veronica said. "I've been watching the weather forecast just to see if we needed to set up two tents or one."

Gertie wheeled around to face them. "Smart thinking. We want to be sure our guests don't get wet if it rains. We've figured out how to set it up so they can flow in and out without getting rained on."

"But for Marly's day, the weather is going to be gorgeous. No rain in sight. So we'll open the wall and have the dance floor flow right into the tent." Veronica pointed outside. "The sides of the tent will stay open, and we will have a bar at each end. That way there will be a view of the water from inside too. Here's a picture." Veronica whipped out her binder and flipped to the sketch she'd done, then turned it toward the two women.

"Excellent. Thank you." Gertie nodded her approval and turned to Marly. "So Marly, is Edward going to join us?"

"He might come in a little bit. He and Jasper had a meeting that ran late."

Veronica couldn't help but notice that Gertie seemed disappointed with Marly's answer. Did she actually *want* to see Edward? Veronica couldn't imagine that, he was so stuffy and formal, not anyone she'd picture Gertie wanting to hang around.

"Shall we go look at some of the desserts? I've had a

sampling set up in one of the small rooms within the kitchen." Veronica directed Marly and Gertie out of the main ballroom and toward the kitchen.

"Oh! Here you guys are!" Sarah's voice rang out from behind them, and they turned to see her hurrying toward them with a giant box in her arms. On the outside was a bright sticker that read "Caution Live Animals."

"What in the hell is that?" Gertie asked, craning her neck.

"Butterflies. Painted lady butterflies, to be exact." Sarah answered nonchalantly as she tapped the box. "Marly wanted them released at the reception when the disc jockey introduces her and Jasper."

"Wait. You want us to keep them until the wedding? We can't!" Veronica said.

Marly fisted her hands on her hips. "You have to. We don't have anywhere else to keep them."

"The wedding isn't for four more days. Butterflies have to remain dormant. That means keeping this box below sixty degrees, but not freezing them. We don't have any place to do that. The freezers and refrigerators are too cold," Veronica said, raising her voice.

"Can't you just put them in the fridge?" Marly raised her voice to match Veronica's.

"No, they'll die! The temperature cannot fluctuate by too much, so the box needs to be monitored."

"Well, then just make sure they are watched over. It's your job as the wedding venue!" Marly practically shouted the last few words.

Gertie frowned at Marly. "We don't have anyone here to babysit butterflies."

"Look, I don't care who babysits them, but it's *your* problem, not mine. Just get it done!" Marly grabbed the box from Sarah, shoved it at Veronica and stormed off.

Veronica stood with the box of butterflies and looked at Gertie.

"Bridezilla has left the building," Gertie muttered under her breath.

Veronica looked around, satisfied that everyone within earshot and anyone lurking in the hall had just witnessed what had happened. Good. Now they all know. She was sure that anyone who wasn't in the room would soon find out about the bridezilla butterfly spat. She knew how people loved to gossip about stuff like that. She walked over to the table and placed the box on top of it.

"I read up on these butterflies," Veronica explained to Gertie loud enough for everyone to hear. "It's critical that this box stays at sixty degrees. No more, no less. If it gets too warm or too cold, they'll die."

"Huh. Well, I guess we could assign someone to

make sure that doesn't happen," Gertie said uncertainly.

Veronica fiddled with the box. "There's a built-in temperature gauge here. It's already increasing!" She ran to the freezer and grabbed several ice packets and placed them strategically around the box, ensuring the ice wasn't touching the sides and was just close enough to bring the temperature down.

"Now what?" Gertie asked, poking at one of the ice blocks. "This thing will melt eventually, you know."

"I'll take care of it, Gertie. Don't worry." Veronica herded Gertie toward the door, not wanting her to decide to hire yet another lost soul whose job would be to babysit the damn butterflies.

Gertie took off toward her office. Veronica bumped into Harper as she turned toward hers.

"Hi! How's everything going?" Harper asked.

"Good. Great, actually. A few bumps here and there, but so far so good." Veronica didn't want to chat right now. She wanted to get to her office. She still had a lot of work to do.

"I passed the bride on her way out. I feel bad for you having to deal with her. She sounds miserable!"

Veronica laughed. "Yeah, well, that's part of my job I guess. Speaking of which, I need to get back to my office. I still have a ton to do before the wedding! It was good seeing you again."

She left Harper and went to her office. She sat down and let out a sigh of relief. They had pulled it off. Now they only needed to see who would mess with the box of butterflies, which was actually just an empty box. TJ had set up a GoPro camera behind a bunch of boxes across from the table the night before. If anyone tampered with the box, they'd know who was messing with the wedding.

She picked up her phone and dialed TJ's extension to tell him the plan was in motion.

HARPER WATCHED Veronica walk away before entering the reception area, her eyes drifting to the butterfly box. She'd heard the argument between Marly and Veronica and immediately spied another opportunity to mess with the wedding. If Uncle Tanner knew about the butterflies, she knew exactly what his instructions would be. Make sure they don't survive.

She stepped closer to the box, looking around first to ensure no one was paying any attention to her. She reached out toward the top of the box, but she couldn't remove it. No matter what Uncle Tanner might want, she just couldn't bring herself to kill anything, even a bunch of butterflies. She had to draw the line somewhere. Best not to tell Uncle Tanner in the first place.

She headed back down to the storage area, guilt over not doing what her uncle would have wanted washing over her. But there was no way she could kill butterflies. Ruining the cake topper had made her feel bad enough. Not to mention that she had had to hide in the storage room for more than an hour to do it. Luckily one only needed a key card to get *in*, not to get out. All she had had to do was slip out after everyone was gone and before the security cameras kicked in at seven. It paid to get friendly with the IT guys when it came to finding out what areas were under surveillance, as well as how to ruin a computer cable and make it look like an accident.

Her phone chirped with an incoming text from Tanner.

Swap out the tags on the tent poles in storage area. Put the red tags on the poles that have green ones and vice versa.

Hm... he wanted her to switch some tags that are on some old poles in the storage area. An odd request, but it didn't sound like it's anything that will hurt someone. Or will it?

Harper stared at the phone for a long time. The other things she'd done had been mean but not anything that would actually hurt anyone. It seemed

Uncle Tanner was getting a little bit more dangerous in his requests.

When he'd asked her to do this favor, she'd never questioned it. She'd always done what he'd asked of her. But now she wasn't so sure. What had she gotten herself into?

17

Veronica was up before the sun and was at work early, excited to review the GoPro results from the night before. She'd tried to track down TJ the day before to tell him how well the staged fight had gone over the butterflies, but he hadn't answered his phone or been in his office. She was a bit disappointed about that, so she'd practically run to his office as soon as she got into the building this morning. He wasn't in.

"Sorry, buddy," she said to her plant as she watered the roots. She'd forgotten to water it again, and it was hanging on by a thread. She heaved it up onto the printer table near the window so that it could catch some of the early morning sun streaming through her windows.

She pulled up the wedding checklist on her

computer. This morning a bunch of deliveries were due, so she headed down to the kitchen to make sure the chef knew about them. She knew he was still experimenting with some of the appetizers. He could become so engrossed in his creations that he might not put the deliveries away. He was an excellent chef, but he wasn't very communicative and often left things until the last minute. Better to make sure someone would be there to tend to the deliveries.

As she left the kitchen and headed back upstairs, she saw Gertie in the lobby speaking with Edward. She waved and kept walking, wondering what they were talking about. Edward sure did seem to like to hang out here.

She settled into her office and started to make some phone calls to ensure that the photographer was all set. Then the band, followed by the guest disc jockey for later in the night. She ensured the head-count was updated and that everyone had RSVPed and was aware of the new location for the reception by sending one final reminder email to all the guests. Thank goodness for technology! This was not a small wedding. If she had had to call everyone, it would have taken a week just to do that!

"Morning." TJ appeared in her doorway, the GoPro stick in his hand. "You ready to check this out?"

"Absolutely," Veronica said, scooting her chair over to make room for him next to her.

He pulled a chair up, and they both looked at the small GoPro screen. Their knees touched as they slowly scrolled through the frames. Veronica found it hard to focus on the footage.

Should she ask him out to lunch? Why not? The new Veronica wanted to be more outgoing and make friends. Just do it, for crying out loud! It's only lunch. Big deal. Say it casually. Just ask!

"So, do you have any..."

"Who is that?" TJ yelled, interrupting her, his attention on the screen.

Veronica jerked her face back toward the screen and saw a young man standing at the box of butterflies. He seemed to be reading the instructions on the side of the box. He looked around, as if to make sure no one was watching, and then slowly removed the lid. He closed it almost immediately, leaned down to look at the thermometer, and moved around the ice blocks surrounding the box. Then he walked away.

"What was he doing? It looked like he was moving the packs away. What if it gets too warm inside the box?" Veronica's heart raced. She thought she recognized the guy from the kitchen staff. "That guy must be connected to Tanner somehow."

"That's Ben. He's part of the kitchen staff. Stay

here. I'm going to go get him." TJ left and returned a few minutes later with Ben.

"What's going on?" Ben asked.

"You tell us." Veronica crossed her arms over her chest. "Why were you screwing around with the butterflies last night?"

Ben looked at them with a confused expression on his face. "Huh?"

"Don't act stupid. We have you on video," TJ said.

"Look, I don't know what the problem is, but I don't work for either of you. I work for Gertie, and I only answer to Gertie. I don't even know who you two are." Ben turned to leave.

"Did I hear my name?" Gertie appeared in the doorway. Her eyes flicked from Veronica to TJ to Ben. "What's going on here?" The frown on her face showed she wasn't happy.

Ben pointed to TJ. "I have no idea. I was prepping food, and this guy comes in and starts talking about butterflies and then brings me up here."

"Gertie, the butterflies were part of a plan to catch whoever was trying to sabotage Marly's wedding. The box is empty. It's filled with tissue paper. We hid a GoPro camera to see who would mess with the box, and it was this kid," TJ explained.

Veronica stood and nodded for support. They hadn't told Gertie about the plan, figuring the fewer people who knew the better. Not to mention that Gertie was already overworked and neither of them wanted her to have something else to worry about.

"What? Good grief. You two should stick to your day jobs. You make really bad detectives. I asked Ben to keep an eye on the butterflies so they didn't croak. The stupid temperature thing. I mean, you do realize the ice packs wouldn't last all night, right? Ben stays overnight here. He was just doing his job!"

Veronica felt like an idiot, especially for not telling Gertie about the plan to begin with. She could tell by Gertie's glare that she was pissed.

"Sorry, Gertie. We were trying to figure out who was trying to ruin the wedding before they do anything else. It worries me," Veronica explained, hoping Gertie would understand.

"I don't really know what you guys are talking about, but it sounds like you're looking for someone shady. If so, you should probably check out the tent poles," Ben said.

Gertie made a face. "Tent poles?"

"I worked for Howard's Party Supply before I came here. We rented out the same tent you have here, the big fancy ones. And one of them collapsed on an entire bar mitzvah party. It was a mess!"

Veronica glanced at TJ. His jawline tightened, but

other than that, there was no evidence of his tent phobia.

"People use tents every day for parties. That must have been a fluke," Veronica said.

"Turns out the poles had rotted inside and buckled under the weight. Some of those poles you have downstairs don't look much better. The ones with the red tags on them look rotted out. I'd check them if I were you. You should never use wooden poles. Use only metal poles."

Everyone stared at him, and he shifted uncomfortably. "Can I go now?"

Gertie flapped her hand at him. "Yes. Go. Thanks for the tip on the poles."

Ben leveled a look at Veronica and TJ before rushing out of the office.

"Well, I guess we need to buy new tent poles," TJ said.

"No, it's fine. We cannot get off of schedule! The tent is going up today. I'll call the place I bought them from and get the story on the poles and which ones to use to make sure it's safe," Gertie replied, waving him off with her hand.

Edward suddenly poked his head into the office. He nodded curtly at Veronica and her stomach soured. He still made her nervous.

"Great job so far, Ms. St. John. It's incredible to think that the wedding is only three days away, but I just looked at the venue, and it has come together nicely." He looked at Gertie. "Are you ready, Gertie? Everyone's here for a final review. And I brought your favorite thing." Grinning, he reached into his suit and pulled out a checkbook, making Gertie giggle like a schoolgirl. She wheeled out of Veronica's office, and Edward followed behind her, leaving Veronica and TJ alone.

"Well, it looks like Gertie is a bit preoccupied with Edward. We need to make sure the tent gets the right poles regardless of what she said. We don't need any more disasters around here," TJ said.

Veronica simply nodded. She was still a bit in shock over Edward's compliment. First Marly acts friendly, then Edward gives her a compliment. All her hard work at being nice was starting to pay off with good karma.

Just as they both started toward the door, Marly popped her head in.

"I just wanted to come by and thank you for fixing everything with my wedding gown. I just came from the fitting, and it's absolutely perfect!" Marly beamed at Veronica and then nodded to TJ. "Okay, I gotta run. We have some food tasting in the kitchen, and I don't want the groom getting antsy. You know how he can be when he's kept waiting! I'll check with you later about Project Butterfly."

Veronica, taken aback by how friendly and sincere Marly was, barely managed to get out "You're welcome" before Marly disappeared.

She looked to TJ. "I guess she'll be disappointed with the results of Project Butterfly."

"No doubt. Don't worry. I'll put the GoPro back and maybe someone else will try to disturb them."

"Maybe. But now I guess we better see to those tent poles before something else goes wrong."

18

The tent lay in a giant heap in the outdoor reception area when Veronica and TJ got there. Gertie had texted her, verifying Ben's story that the green-tagged poles were the ones to use. Knowing his thing with tents, she'd told him he didn't have to go with her, but he'd insisted. He said he had a vested interest in making sure things went well too, and that they were in this together.

Veronica eyed the heap of canvas and poles, noticing a red tag on one of the poles.

"Excuse me," she said as she grabbed the closest worker by the arm. "The poles with red tags on them should *not* be used for the tent. The poles with the green tags are the right ones."

"Huh? Look, lady, I was just told to grab the poles, and these were the ones I found," the worker replied nonchalantly, not seeming to care too much about what Veronica had said.

"Hey! *Listen.* I said use the *green*-tagged poles. Not the ones with red tags. I'm the one responsible for managing this wedding! Got it?" Veronica's yelling caused the workers within earshot to stop and stare.

"Okay, okay. Geez. Sorry, lady," the worker mumbled and called over several other employees, telling them they needed to go get the poles with the green tags.

Veronica turned around to see TJ staring at her, laughing. "What?"

"*That* was the Veronica I remember from the cooking contest. I was wondering when she would show up."

"Ha! Well, I'm trying to be less bossy, but this needs to be done the right way. It's a good thing we came down here to tell them, or they would have used the wrong poles, and that would have wasted a lot of time."

"Agreed, great job." TJ held his hand up for a high five.

Veronica slapped his hand, and their eyes locked.

"Hey, how about we go out after work and celebrate?" His voice was lower, more serious now. "I mean, you owe me dinner anyway, don't you?"

Veronica laughed, glad that he had made a small joke out of it so there wasn't a lot of "this is a date" pressure.

"You're on. I'll swing by your office when I'm done here. Sound good?" she asked him as a few employees walked past, struggling with the giant tent poles.

"Sounds good. See you then."

Veronica watched TJ walk away and did a little victory pump as some of the employees walking by gave her a strange look.

"Pay attention to that tent, not me!" she said to them, too happy to let their dirty looks burst her bubble. The dinner probably meant nothing, but at the very least, TJ liked her and wanted to spend time with her. If nothing else, he could be a friend. And Veronica was finding out she dearly wanted some friends.

She stood and watched as the crew started to erect the tent, paying close attention to the poles to ensure they used the right ones. Satisfied that they were on the right track, she headed back to her office, her thoughts on Ben and the butterflies. Ben had been the only one caught on the GoPro, which meant no one else tried to do anything with the box. But, surely, if Tanner's minion was around, he or she would have done something. Maybe Gertie had been right when she'd said they didn't have to worry about Tanner anymore. Just what had Gertie said to him?

Veronica's mood had improved immensely. Even though the saboteur might still be on the loose, she'd thwarted another disaster and had plans for dinner. Best of all, Marly was happy! Things were all falling into place.

As she passed Gertie's office, she heard a familiar man's voice. She stopped and leaned back toward Gertie's door so she could hear what was being said and try to determine who it was she was talking to.

"Well, now that everything is taken care of, how about going to dinner with me tonight to celebrate?"

"Oh, I can't, dear. Thank you, though. I have to go meet Tanner Durcotte at one of his restaurants. We have some business to discuss. Maybe another time?"

Veronica froze. She recognized the voice. It was Edward! He had just asked Gertie out to dinner, and she had said no because she was meeting Tanner! What the hell was going on here?

She continued toward her office, shaking her head. She made a mental note to tell Gertie to stay away from both Tanner and Edward when she could talk to her alone.

She slipped back into her office and pushed the door half shut. Even the plant on her printer table was looking up. It was slowly coming back to life, some new bright green leaves sprouting off of one of the branches.

She leaned over to pull it closer to the window for more sun, and while doing so caught a glimpse of something on the street below.

The man wore a red shirt, the same color TJ had been wearing earlier today. Wait a minute. It *was* TJ. He was talking to someone familiar. Wait! It was Sarah.

Veronica leaned forward to get a better view, her face smashed against the window, just in time to catch TJ giving Sarah a hug and a kiss and then climb into a car with her. Her heart plummeted. TJ was dating Sarah?

She stepped back, her arm catching on a branch of the plant. It fell, and the soil spilled all over the shiny floor.

"Dammit!" she yelled as she started to scoop up the dirt with her hands.

"Uh-oh, that didn't sound good. Need some help in here?" Harper had been lurking outside Veronica's office when she heard the plant hit the floor.

"Stupid plant!" Veronica mumbled as she scooped

up the last remaining lumps of dirt and threw them back into the pot. "I knew I'd end up killing it."

"C'mon." Harper said. "Take a break for a few minutes. You need to wash those hands anyway."

Veronica stood and held her dirt-smudged hands in front of her. "Yeah, good idea. I could use a break."

They headed to the break room. Veronica made a bee-line for the sink, and Harper headed to the vending machine. "What do you want? My treat."

"M&Ms would be great. No, wait, Peppermint Patty. Oh screw it, M&Ms are fine. Thanks."

Harper pushed the buttons on the machine, and it whirred into action, spitting out two packages of the candy. She handed one bag to Veronica as she sat at the table. The room was empty. There was a big break room downstairs and because most of the staff worked on the first floor, it was used more frequently.

"So, how's the wedding planning going?" Harper sensed that something was wrong, and she wanted to know what it was, so she could report back to Tanner.

"Ugh. I mean, it's fine. It's just so stressful. Keeping Marly happy, making sure Gertie is happy, ensuring I'm not going over TJ's *stupid* budget. And doing it all in record time."

"I'm sure it's crazy, trying to keep everyone happy," Harper said, unsure exactly why Veronica called TJ's budget stupid. It sounded more as if she was angry with him rather than something to do with the wedding. "Was TJ's budget way off or something?"

Veronica shrugged. "I guess not. I mean, whatever. He's just not who I thought he was. He seemed like a nice guy, but I think he's just a jerk like the rest of them, know what I mean? One minute he's great, and the next minute he's a jerk."

Harper knew exactly what she meant but remained silent as she watched Veronica pick through the bag of M&M's. Did Veronica have a crush on TJ? If anyone knew what it felt like to be screwed over by a crush, it was Harper.

She'd been cheated on by her fiancé, and it had been horrible. She'd been blindsided and had had to call off her wedding less than a month before they were set to walk down the aisle. It had been humiliating.

Thank God for Uncle Tanner coming to her rescue, keeping her cheered up, and taking care of everything for her. He had always been so good to her, but now she had to admit she was starting to have doubts about his plans to ruin this wedding. Truth was, she was a little worried about the tags she'd switched on those tent poles.

"Yeah, I don't date much these days. I think I'm better off just focusing on work for now," Harper said, hesitant to tell Veronica about her failed engagement.

It was humiliating telling people she had been cheated on, so she avoided talking about it as much as possible.

"Ha! I don't date ever! I've only had one relationship, and that was enough for me. It was a nightmare. He was a cheater and a liar. I'd rather work too. I'm actually happy that this job eats up so much time. It keeps me busy," Veronica said, folding up the half-eaten bag of M&Ms.

"He cheated?" Harper asked, immediately feeling a bond with Veronica. "Mine did too. It kind of makes you lose your trust in people, doesn't it?"

"Yes! It totally does. Sorry that you were cheated on too. At least we're both better off now."

"Definitely better off now." Harper smiled at Veronica. Suddenly the other woman didn't seem the mean bitch Tanner had portrayed. She seemed nice. And they had things in common that made Harper feel they could even be friends. Well, until Veronica discovered the role Harper played in sabotaging the wedding. But, so far all those things had been fixed, and the wedding was almost here. Maybe Uncle Tanner wouldn't have anything more for her to wreck.

"So, do you have a lot left to do for the wedding? I mean, I know there must be, but it seems like things are falling into place for you from what I've seen around here," Harper said.

"Well, there's some weird stuff that's been

happening around here with the wedding. Almost like someone is trying to sabotage it. Earlier I was told that some of the tent poles have rot in them. There are two sets of poles, and the wrong ones were being used. I mean, can you imagine that huge tent falling down on top of everyone? I have a ton of candles that will be under that tent. It could easily catch fire if it collapsed."

"That would have been horrible!" Harper was shocked. So that's why Uncle Tanner had wanted her to switch the tags on the tent poles. He wanted the tent to collapse.

Suddenly she felt sick. People could get hurt. So now who was the monster, Veronica or Uncle Tanner?

"So, you're sure the tent poles that are being used now are the right ones?" she asked cautiously.

"Yes. I called the person Gertie bought them from and found out that the green-tagged poles are the right ones, not the red-tagged ones," Veronica replied. "I watched them start to set the tent up to make sure it was okay."

"Oh, cool." Panic bubbled up. She had already swapped out the tags on the poles as Uncle Tanner had told her to do. So now the green-tagged poles were probably the bad ones, assuming that's why Tanner had wanted her to switch them. "Well, I should get back to work, I guess. I still have a lot of stuff to do for Gertie. You know how she is if you fall behind."

"Yeah. Thanks for the chat." Veronica waved as Harper rushed out of the room.

Harper ran out the door and down the stairs toward the outdoor reception area. She needed to check the tent poles.

"What's going on?" she asked Bob, one of the maintenance guys, as she maneuvered around the tent poles that were now strewn around the lawn.

"We're changing the poles on the tent. Something about some of them being unstable or something, I don't know." Bob sounded irritated. "Hm. Well, that's what I came to check on. You should be using the ones with the red tags. Not the green ones." She reached down and pointed at a pole with a green tag.

The pole in Bob's hand clattered to the floor, and he turned to face Harper. He did not look happy. "Look, someone else just told us an hour ago that we had to use the poles with green tags. Now you come along and say use the red-tagged ones. Can someone make up their mind? We have other stuff to do!"

"Red tags! Use the poles with the red tags. And if anyone else comes along and tries to change it, you tell them Gertie said use the red tags!"

Bob's brows flew up. "Okay. Sheesh. Don't get your panties in a wad."

She stood with her arms crossed and waited for them to start swapping the poles out, ensuring that they used those with the red tags. Her heart filled with regret.

She'd come to like working for Gertie. The old lady was feisty and kind and smart. She even reminded her of Auntie Emily a bit. She looked a lot like her from a certain angle. And after talking to Veronica, now Harper knew she wasn't as horrible as Uncle Tanner had made her out to be. She didn't know what Uncle Tanner's issue was, but she did know that Veronica wasn't the person Uncle Tanner pictured.

Veronica and Gertie deserved for this wedding reception to go off without a hitch, and if that meant Uncle Tanner would be angry with her because she'd made sure that this tent wasn't going to crumble down on top of everyone, then so be it.

TANNER STRAIGHTENED his tie in front of the mirror. He supposed he wasn't too bad looking. His hair, or what was left of it, had that salt-and-pepper look, and he wasn't too grossly overweight. He stepped back and smoothed the suit jacket. It was his best suit. For some strange reason, he wanted to look good for his dinner with Gertie.

He'd spent most of the day eagerly awaiting the dinner. For the first time since Emily had died, he was actually looking forward to something. And for the first time in a long time, he discovered that someone's opinion of him mattered. Gertie's opinion.

After he'd met her in his restaurant, she'd called him, and they'd talked on the phone for a long time. What about, exactly, he could not recall. He remembered only that her voice was soothing, her words made sense. Unlike most of the people he'd met in his businesses, she didn't judge him. She restored some of the hopeful feelings he'd had years ago.

What had happened to make him so bitter and angry? Life had beaten him down, but as Gertie had pointed out, that was no reason for him to try to bring others down. Look at Gertie and all the obstacles she'd had to overcome. It made him feel ashamed that he'd resorted to bringing others down when Gertie had much more challenging obstacles to overcome and did so while remaining positive and even working hard to help others.

Tanner remembered the last text he'd sent to Harper about the tent poles. He almost wished he hadn't done that. It would ruin the wedding, and if the wedding was ruined, Gertie would be ruined. Or maybe not. Maybe Gertie would be okay. It was just one event. Marly might not be too happy, but she deserved that, right? And Veronica too.

But Tanner didn't feel exactly like that was right anymore. Maybe he should text Harper and call off the pole-switching. Nah, better to wait until after dinner. No need to make any drastic decisions right this minute.

19

Veronica stared at the empty M&M wrapper in her trash barrel. Stupid candy. That was pretty much her only vice. Well, that and now the lip balm. At least lip balm didn't have any calories! She would have to spend extra time working out to burn off those M&Ms or make one hundred extra trips up and down the stairs here at the office.

She wished she hadn't eaten them but was glad that she had had Harper to talk to. She congratulated herself on cleverly trying to wangle information out of Harper by mentioning the tentpole incident. She'd wanted to see if Harper knew of anyone suspicious who might be causing the problems, but she'd seemed clueless, so Veronica hadn't learned anything.

She kind of liked Harper. She seemed really down-to-earth, and they actually had a few things in common. Veronica had never had many friends. Or any, for that matter. She had typically kept to herself her whole life. The other kids had teased her mercilessly when she was growing up, so as an adult, she had developed defenses to push people away.

Maybe it was time for her to stop being so stand-offish when it came to making friends. It seemed she might enjoy being friends with Harper and maybe even Marly. Not TJ, though.

She checked the soil in her office plant. She'd put all the dirt back and packed it in. The plant seemed none the worse for it. Luckily the pot was plastic and hadn't broken. She avoided looking out the window, afraid of whom or what she might see below this time. She had seen enough earlier!

She glanced down at her watch. It was almost time to go home. She had spent a few hours updating spreadsheets for the wedding and looking out her office door more than she probably should have. Every time she had heard footsteps in the hallway, her heart had skipped a beat. Was it TJ?

But it hadn't been. Her "date" with him obviously wasn't going to happen because he apparently was still with Sarah. She was being stood up. She shut down her computer and let out a heavy sigh.

Wait. What if she bumped into TJ on her way out

of the building? What if he was standing there, kissing Sarah? That would be so awkward. She grabbed her purse and decided to leave through one of the side doors to avoid him.

She exited her office and briskly walked down the hallway to the elevator.

Ding!

Shoot! Someone was getting off! She ducked into an empty office, cautiously pulling the door almost shut behind her. She didn't want to risk seeing TJ if he was in the elevator. She left the door open a crack to see if she could hear anything or catch a glimpse of who it was.

The elevator doors slid open and voices filled the hallway. She recognized Gertie's voice immediately. But who was the man with her? His voice sounded really familiar, but she was having a hard time placing it. She listened for another minute. Wait. It was Tanner Durcotte!

"As always, I enjoyed our talk Gertie. When will I see you again?"

"I'm busy with this wedding stuff the next few days. I'll be in touch, though. Now remember what we talked about. I don't need you to walk me to my office. Thank you, sweetie!"

Veronica peeked out from behind the door and saw Tanner standing in the hallway watching Gertie wheel away. She pulled back inside as he turned to get back into the elevator, but not before she saw the goofy lovestruck look on his face. What the hell was going on around here?

She'd forgotten to warn Gertie about Tanner, and now they'd been out on what appeared to be a date. The last thing she needed was a confrontation with Tanner right now, so she stayed put until she heard the elevator doors swoosh shut.

As soon as she heard the elevator start, she came out of hiding and hurried to the window. She wanted to make sure Tanner actually was leaving. By the way he'd looked at Gertie, she didn't doubt he might double back inside, and she didn't want to cross paths with him.

Tanner didn't come back inside, but he didn't leave either. Instead of getting into a cab, he walked around toward the gated side of the building that led to the back reception area. She watched as he punched in the code and opened the gate, looking around quickly before he disappeared behind the fence.

Who gave him the code to the gate? Certainly not Gertie. Then her heart jerked in her chest. If it was Tanner who had been messing around with the wedding, then he had a contact inside. That person could have given him the code. And now Tanner was in the reception area, where they'd just finished setting up the tent.

Veronica rushed to the elevator and mashed her thumb into the button repeatedly. She needed to get down there before Tanner ruined something else.

HARPER ORDERED her second beer and leaned back on the barstool, relieved that the right tent poles were being used. Luckily she had talked to Veronica or something really bad could have happened. The tent was so huge that if it collapsed on all those people, someone was bound to get hurt. She couldn't live with herself if that happened.

She sipped her beer, and her phone went off, signaling an incoming text from Tanner. Her stomach knotted. She had hoped that he was done with all this "let's ruin the wedding" stuff after not hearing from him in a while.

I can't go through with ruining the wedding. It's wrong. I'm going to make it right tonight.

Good. He'd finally come to his senses. Wait, what did he mean by "make it right?" What was he planning to do tonight? Usually he had her do all his dirty work because she had access to most of the building... wait, she'd given him the code to the outdoor area. That wouldn't get him in to the building, though.

She sent a quick text asking what he was talking about and then stared at her phone for the answer while her anxiety ratcheted higher.

He wasn't answering. This was not good.

The code she'd given him led to the outdoor reception area. The one where the tent was. He must be thinking that the rotted poles are still being used to support the tent. He doesn't know that she's already switched them. She had to stop him before he switched them back!

20

TJ rushed back into the building. He didn't want to be late for his date with Veronica. He didn't have any work to do that afternoon and had just tagged along with Sarah, Marly, and Jasper on an errand. They had taken longer than he had expected. He didn't know Marly and Jasper that well, and he'd enjoyed getting to know them better. Plus, any time he could spend with his sister was time well spent, especially after all the time they'd wasted apart. A big topic of discussion had been Veronica, and TJ was happy that Marly and Sarah were starting to warm toward her. Still, when he'd mentioned that he needed to get back because he was having dinner with her, Sarah had seemed dubious. Oh well, he was sure Veronica would win her over in time.

He passed two employees in the hallway who were talking about the tent. Just thinking about that thing gave him the willies. And then it made him feel guilty. He wanted to attend the wedding to support Gertie and Veronica, but there was no way he was going anywhere near that tent. Just the sight of it thrust his anxiety through the roof. He'd almost bolted out of the area earlier today when he'd gone down with Veronica, and it was only by sheer force of will that he'd stayed while she'd bossed the maintenance crew around about those poles.

Thinking about Veronica bossing them around brought a smile to his face. He got a kick out of her when she got that way. Working with her on this project, though, he'd gotten to see the other side of her. She was smart and funny and sweet, even under that bitchy persona she tried to project.

He hurried along the hallway, anxious to get their date underway. Did Veronica think it was a date, though? He wasn't sure. It had been so long since TJ had actually dated he wasn't sure he knew the signs anymore. He'd have to play it by ear.

He peeked inside Veronica's office. Empty. Had she gone to the break room or downstairs? No, her purse was gone from the hook where it usually hung, and her computer was shut off. Disappointment swelled in his chest.

Had she left without him?

He was a few minutes late, but surely she could have waited. Unless she didn't want to go out with him. Right, that was probably it. She probably didn't want to go out with him and didn't know how to turn him down as that would make things awkward at work.

He couldn't blame her. Why would someone as smart and put-together as Veronica want to get involved with someone who had been a drug addict?

He turned around and started down the hall, his shoulders slumped. He should have known better than to hope his feelings for Veronica would be reciprocated.

TANNER PUSHED the heavy plastic table up against the gate, blocking it. There! Now no one could interrupt him.

He walked toward the tent, taken aback by its enormity. He probably should have asked Harper to help him, but he had already involved her enough in all of this. Ellen wouldn't have appreciated that. No, he had no one but himself to blame for this, and he had to fix it himself.

He couldn't take back what he had done, but hopefully he could make some of it right. And that included asking Harper to do these mean things. If anyone tried to blame her, he would take that blame himself. From here on, he was going to do what was right, starting with fixing the tent poles.

After this, he would try to make restitution for all of the bad things he'd done. After his dinner with Gertie, he'd realized that his actions were a reaction to his pain over the loss of Ellen. That was wrong. And besides, he no longer felt the need to lash out.

That was because of Gertie. Now that she was in his life, he had a spark of hope for happiness. If he'd had any doubts about his actions before their dinner, he had none now. He was ready to let go of his vengeful thoughts and move forward.

But the tent was huge, and he had no idea how he could switch the poles out alone.

He poked around at one of the poles, trying to loosen it by rocking it back and forth. Humph. They were pretty sturdy for rotted-out poles.

Maybe they would be fine? No. He needed to make sure that the right poles were used or else who knew what could happen. And if something bad did happen, his new friend Gertie would suffer.

Gertie was a very special woman. He could talk to her without masking his feelings. Gertie was an amazing woman, and she deserved the best. All the crappy things he'd done to ruin Marly's wedding hurt Gertie because they reflected on her new business. Tanner simply could not have that. He was going to right this wrong, no matter the cost.

VERONICA RAN down the stairs and out the side exit that was closest to the outer gate. She entered the code, pushing on the door.

It wouldn't open! She threw her shoulder against it, using all of her weight.

It didn't budge. Tanner must have jammed it with something on the other side so no one could get in.

She turned around and sprinted back to the side door, only to realize that it was locked. She pulled out her key card, forgetting that this door didn't have key-card access.

"Dammit!" She ran back to the front entrance. She had been hoping to avoid being inside the building in case TJ and Sarah showed up, but she needed to get to that tent to stop Tanner.

She tried to pull the door open only to find it locked. It must be past five; the automatic locks were on. She grabbed her key card and swiped it, finally gaining access to the building.

She ran toward the reception area. She could see

the interior reception area through the large glass door, and beyond that, the glass wall with the tent just outside. As she ran to the door, the tent swayed precariously.

It was dark outside, and if it wasn't for the candles flickering in the glass box luminaries that lit the pathway from the tent to the seating area at the edge of the river, she might not have seen the dark figure under the tent.

Tanner was doing something to the tent. But what? Was he trying to take it down? Maybe he was trying to weaken the poles so that it collapsed during the reception.

She slammed her key card into the inner-door reader, pushed the door open and rushed to the sliding glass wall. It was already unlocked! Tanner must have known the keypad combination that unlocked it from outside. She pulled the door open and ran into reception area under the tent, stumbling over a pile of tent poles.

"What the *hell* do you think you are doing?" Veronica's voice was a bit breathless from all the running.

Tanner was in the center of the tent, fumbling around with the large pole. He stopped and looked over at her, sweat dripping from his forehead. "I'm trying to fix this. I don't want to mess up the wedding!"

Veronica half laughed, half choked. "You think I believe that! Don't forget, I know how nasty you can be." She stormed over and pushed him away from the pole.

"No! You don't understand. These poles are faulty. They're rotted!" Tanner jogged to the end of the tent and started fiddling with another pole.

"You're too late. We already figured that out and switched them, so you're little plan backfired." Veronica reached for her phone to call Gertie or the police, anyone who would come and help her stop Tanner. But then she heard flapping and looked up to see that Tanner had the pole out of the ground, and the side of the tent was collapsing inward.

Veronica threw her phone down and ran to put the pole back into the ground, fumbling with the heavy canvas that was trying to wrap itself around her.

"What? No, you haven't. These are the wrong poles!" Tanner had gone back to the pole in the middle. If nothing else, he was persistent. "I had the good poles swapped out for the bad ones. It was a mistake! I need to make this right and fix it!"

"You switched the tags?" Veronica glanced at one of the poles. Red tags. Hadn't she had the maintenance crew use the green-tagged poles?

At the thick middle pole, Tanner cursed and started to shimmy up the pole. "I know you don't trust me, but I need to make this right. I can't let Gertie suffer."

"No, wait!" Veronica didn't trust Tanner, but something odd was going on here. If he had switched the tags as he claimed, then the green-tagged poles were the ones that were rotted, which meant the red-tagged poles were good. She had no idea how the tent had been erected with those poles when she'd expressly told the crew to use those with green tags, but if Tanner was right the current poles were the good ones.

Tanner was at the top, clutching onto the canvas fabric. "Get out! I'm bringing it down. I gotta get rid of these poles."

"No!" Veronica jumped onto the pole. "The poles are the right ones. You'll ruin the tent!"

If the tent was ruined, Marly's wedding would be ruined. She shimmied up toward Tanner.

"These are the wrong poles! They will snap in half!" Tanner yelled, as the pole started to list.

Maybe shimmying up to stop him wasn't such a good idea.

"*Stop it!*" Veronica screamed. "I don't believe you. All you've done is try to ruin people's lives, and I'm not going to let you ruin this wedding!"

She grabbed his ankle and yanked.

Tanner's grip on the canvas tightened.

The pole tilted further and then…

Crash!

The pole ripped out of the ground, and the entire tent came down on top of Veronica, trapping her and Tanner in a heavy layer of canvas.

21

Harper raced to the gate at the side of the building in an attempt to stop whatever it was that Tanner wanted to "make right." He hadn't replied to her text, so she'd thrown money at the bartender and ran to the office to stop him. If it was true that he wanted to make things right, then she guessed he'd switch the tent poles, not knowing that she'd already gone against his previous order and made sure that the good poles were used.

The gate wouldn't open. Something was jammed against it.

Harper jumped up to look over, her heart clenching when she saw the tent sway, then collapse to the ground like a deflated hot-air balloon.

Did she hear muffled yelling? Uncle Tanner might

be trapped!

She grabbed her key card and raced to the front door. She needed to get to the tent via the reception room. She yanked on the door as soon as the lock clicked and ran down the hall, colliding with TJ, who had just come off of the elevator.

He put his hands on her shoulders to steady her. "Whoa, what's the rush?"

"The tent. Outside. The one for Marly's wedding." Harper said in frantic huffs, trying to catch her breath.

"Okay, the tent? Yeah, it's all set up already. I saw it earlier. It looks great," TJ replied, giving her a strange look.

Harper knew she must sound crazy and took a deep breath, trying to calm herself.

"The tags on the tent poles were switched. My Uncle Tanner doesn't realize that the right tent poles are up. He thinks they are the wrong ones, and he's trying to take them down. And I just saw the tent collapse!"

TJ's eyes widened as Harper spoke. She broke free and ran for the stairs, TJ on her heels.

"Hurry!" Harper yelled, taking the stairs two at a time.

They pushed into the ballroom where Harper could see directly through the glass. The tent spread over the ground, almost flat except for two figures in the middle struggling to get out. Uncle Tanner and... she didn't have time to figure out who else was flailing around in there because she saw flames licking the edge of the tent. It had fallen on one of the luminaries lighting the pathway to the river.

"FIRE!" Harper raced to the flames and started stomping on burning canvas.

TJ remained frozen in place, the memory of his tent fire twisting his gut. The thick smoke choking him, the smell of burning canvas, the pain as the flames scorched his skin. The sound of his screams. But now they mingled with other screams, screams coming from under the canvas.

Veronica! She hadn't stood him up. She'd been down here, trying to make sure nothing happened to the tent.

His heart twisted. Veronica was trapped under the heavy canvas. Harper was trying to keep the fire from spreading, but if she didn't, Veronica and whoever was under there with her—Tanner, he assumed —might burn.

"Hold on!" he yelled, lifting enough of the canvas to crawl beneath it.

Inside it was pitch-black. The heavy canvas

engulfed him, grabbing at him on all sides. He couldn't see a thing. TJ's breath came in short gasps, the stifling memories of his tent fire creeping back into his mind. Under the canvas, the air was already stale and heavy. He took a deep breath but couldn't fill his lungs. Dizziness washed over him.

"Get off me, you stupid tent! Gah!"

Veronica's voice brought TJ to the present. A smile tugged at his lips, chasing away the dread and fear. Leave it to her to boss the tent around.

"Veronica! Where are you?!" he yelled, crawling with his arms out in front of him to push the canvas out of his path.

"Hey, who's there? How the hell do I get out of here?" A man's voice yelped out in the dark. It must be Tanner, TJ thought.

"Keep moving this way. Follow my voice." TJ heard the canvas rustling and another sound—hopefully not the fire eating away at it. He didn't dare mention that to Veronica or Tanner lest they panic. Better to remain calm and lead them out.

The tent space around him opened, and Veronica appeared. She was on her hands and knees, her white slacks grass stained, but the smile that lit her face when she saw him made his heart leap. Then a heavy man crawled into the cleared area, causing her to scowl.

"This is your fault!" Veronica accused.

"I was trying to do right. I know I did bad things, but this time I was trying to make things right."

"Huh, I doubt that you—"

"Guys," TJ struggled to keep his voice calm. "Let's focus on getting out. Then you can argue."

"Good idea," the man said.

"Fine." Veronica squinted into the darkness. "Which way is out?"

"Follow me." TJ turned back the way he'd come, using his arms to clear the tent folds in front of him, his legs burning with the weight.

He pushed along inside the tent for what seemed an eternity, eventually seeing some light in the distance. Harper held up a portion of the tent and yelled to them.

TJ cautiously made his way toward the light, pushing the canvas in front of him so Veronica could get out first, then Tanner, who emerged from the tent and jumped up, his arms flailing as if he were being attacked by hundreds of bugs. Finally TJ climbed out, glancing nervously toward where the fire had been, his shoulders relaxing when he saw it was extinguished.

"Uncle Tanner, are you okay?" Harper hugged Tanner.

TJ and Veronica looked at each other, then jerked

their heads back to Tanner and Harper.

Veronica rounded on the girl. "*Uncle* Tanner?! So, *you* were the mole!"

"No, no!" Tanner said quickly as he wiped his forehead and tried to straighten his clothes. "Harper did nothing. It was all me."

Harper shot Tanner a confused look, and Veronica's narrowed glare told TJ she didn't believe Tanner. Before either girl could say anything, Gertie's squeaky wheels interrupted them.

"What the hell is going on here? You damned people ruined the tent!" Gertie yelled as she surveyed the giant mess on the lawn.

"Tanner tried to ruin the wedding! He was trying to switch the poles," Veronica said.

"No, no! I had a change of heart! I came here to replace the bad poles with the good ones. The poles that are up have the red tags." Tanner gestured to a pile of poles on the patio. "I was going to replace them with these green-tagged poles. The good poles."

"What? You're lying. You must have already switched them," Veronica said.

"No. I was here for only a few minutes. I got the good poles and then was going to switch them and hope that no one noticed. You have to believe me." He turned to Gertie, a lovesick look on his face. "Yes, I tried to ruin the wedding by doing other things, but since getting to know Gertie I've had a change of heart. I swear I only wanted to make it right this time."

Gertie chuckled. Leave it to Gertie to laugh when someone was trying to ruin things for her. She wheeled in front of Veronica.

"What did I tell you, Veronica? You catch more flies with honey than you do with vinegar. I knew Tanner would come around. There was no need for you to go off on all those covert missions."

"But he didn't... I mean he was trying to..." Veronica looked from Gertie to the tent poles to Tanner. TJ noticed that Tanner actually did look apologetic. Had Gertie's influence really turned him around?

Gertie spun around to look at the collapsed tent. One corner was slightly singed, but no one would notice that when the sides were rolled up. Near as TJ could tell, the tent remained useable.

"And as far as this tent mess goes, you people better get it set back up pronto! Are you all dense?" Gertie gestured to the pile of poles. "There's nothing wrong with any of these poles. I had them all replaced after we talked to Ben. You don't think I'd have rotted poles just lying around do you? You people all need to step up your game! Get to it!"

Veronica was speechless as she watched Gertie smile at Tanner as if he were a star pupil. How could she just forgive him so easily? He'd almost managed to ruin their first event, which could have spelled the demise of O'Rourke Signature Events!

But Gertie was like that. She never passed judgment. And she always gave a person room to make up for bad deeds. She'd looked past Veronica's antics from the island show and given her this opportunity.

Veronica glanced at Harper and Tanner. She wasn't so sure she could be as generous with her forgiveness as Gertie had been. And as far as Harper, well, she wasn't so sure that she was innocent in this mess.

She suddenly realized that TJ's arm was around her shoulders. Her stomach fluttered. TJ had risked getting stuck under the tent to get her out. No one except Gertie had ever gone out of their way for her. But then she remembered seeing TJ kiss Sarah and she stepped way, looking down at the ground.

"What's wrong?" TJ asked.

Veronica crossed her arms over her chest. "You probably shouldn't have your arm around me if you're seeing someone." It came out sounding a bit childish, but she didn't care.

"Huh? What are you talking about?"

"Sarah Thomas," Veronica said, looking him straight in the eye. She wasn't going to let him get out of this one. She had learned this the hard way with her ex when she'd caught him lying. He'd always played dumb. She didn't think TJ was the type to do that, but the confused look on his face told her otherwise. She knew what she'd seen.

"Ha! You dimwit! Sarah is his sister! Ha ha! Now I've had all the entertainment I can stand for today!" Gertie said.

Veronica was confused. Gertie was wrong.

"They have different last names." She turned to TJ. "And if she's his sister, why didn't he say anything?"

TJ's brow quirked up. "Um… she is my sister. We have a different last name because I needed to protect my family when I was going through those hard years. And what do you mean, why didn't I tell you? Why would I tell you? It wasn't really relevant to anything. And besides, I figured Gertie had already told you."

"Well, she didn't," Veronica said lamely. Now she felt childish *and* stupid. TJ probably thought she was a jerk. Worse, judging by the look on his face, jumping to conclusions about what she'd seen between TJ and Sarah might have ruined things between them.

"Well, this has been fun, but I need everyone to focus on this wedding now! All's well that ends well. Chop, chop! Get this tent up! We have a wedding in two days!" Gertie wheeled off, leaving the rest of them scurrying.

22

V eronica dabbed at her eyes with a tissue. She had spent years trying to make Marly cry, and now here she was, crying at Marly's wedding.

The bride looked stunning. The wedding gown was beyond gorgeous. People had gasped when Marly walked down the aisle at the church. The gown was an off-the-shoulder style with an open back nipped in at the waist and then flared out, with the bottom tapering down in the back. The train was about six feet long. The dazzling Swarovski crystals that had been painstakingly sewn into the gown shimmered and sparkled magnificently as Marly walked down the aisle. It was simple yet elegant, and it fit Marly like a glove. She was glowing, one of the most beautiful brides Veronica had ever seen.

Surprised to even receive an invitation to the ceremony, Veronica had arrived at the church early to make sure Marly had everything she needed. Much to her surprise, Marly had actually hugged her when they first saw each other in the church dressing room. Even Sarah had shot a tentative smile in her direction.

Still, Veronica didn't feel like a part of the gang, so she sat in the last pew. Then, just as the ceremony was ending, she ran out to make sure the limo driver knew where he was taking the bride and groom for photos before the reception. Then she hailed a cab to O'Rourke's to ensure everything was ready for the guests.

The final result in the ballroom at O'Rourke's was nothing short of amazing. The weather had cooperated with a gorgeous evening, so the rear wall of sliding glass had been opened, allowing a slight breeze in. The tables were all set with crisp white linen tablecloths and lilac cloth napkins. White plates with a thin gold line around them sat atop vibrant gold chargers at each setting. Every table had an amazing floral centerpiece of lilac roses and daises. The vases were a unique turquoise glass, something she'd found last minute in storage. She had been worried about the color, but they added a stunning pop to each table.

The sides of the tent were rolled up to afford a better

view of the river, so the singed part wasn't noticeable. The glass luminaries—their doors closed to contain the flickering candles—added an ambiance to the outdoor area that would be magical once the sun set. They'd moved the luminaries further away from the tent upon Gertie's instruction. Apparently someone had placed them too close. Veronica had to wonder if that had been just another part of the plan to ruin the wedding.

The soothing trickle of the wall fountain echoed across the room. None of the guests had arrived, but the servers rushed around dressed in their uniforms of black pants and white button-down shirts, with a lilac rose pinned to their shirts. Veronica had added the lilac rose at the last minute, earning added praise from Gertie.

Veronica walked around, checking things over one last time. In the kitchen, she ran into Harper. She still wasn't sure what to think of the girl. Tanner had insisted she wasn't the one who had been trying to ruin the wedding, but the way Harper turned red when he'd said it made Veronica think he was covering. Veronica had found out later that Harper had insisted they use the red-tagged tent poles and had known that Tanner had had them switched out, so she did have that in her favor. Maybe Veronica should be more like Gertie and show forgiveness.

"Veronica, oh my goodness!" Harper exclaimed when she saw her. "You look amazing!"

Veronica smiled and spun, holding her arms in the air as she did so. A few of the kitchen employees did a low wolf whistle, making her blush. It had been a long time since she'd felt she looked pretty, but the cream-colored dress with its intricately beaded bodice and flowing lines really did flatter her figure and skin tone.

"Thanks! It's a dress from Marly's line. She insisted I try it on the other day, even brought it here for me. Can you believe how great it fits?!" She ran her hands along her sides as she said it, emphasizing her curves. "You don't look so bad yourself."

"Thanks." Harper blushed. Her deep purple tea-length dress was simple, the only adornments teardrop-shaped crystals that hung from the bottom of the jacket. It looked elegant even with Harper pulling the edges of the jacket close as if to hide inside the dress. "I feel awkward being dressed up. I mean, I don't even know Marly or Jasper."

"Gertie wanted all of us to attend the first event here. It's a big deal. Is everything all set with the butterflies? I mean, for real this time?" Veronica asked. She had arranged for real butterflies to be released during Jasper and Marly's first dance.

"Yes, everything is perfect. Marly will love it," Harper said.

"Great. Well, I guess everything is ready. The guests should start to arrive, and Marly and Jasper will be here soon. We should go into the reception room."

In the ballroom, Gertie was talking to Tanner at one of the bars. She caught Veronica's eye and motioned her and Harper over.

"Oh, girls! You look so beautiful!"

Both of them slowed as they neared Tanner and got a full view of Gertie.

"Gertie?" They both exclaimed, not believing what they were seeing. Gertie wore a strapless, long beige dress. Her skin was bronze, and her long arms were extremely toned. She had her long grey hair pulled up in a very tight bun, with a few loose strands framing her face. Her green eyes stood out against her bronzed skin, and her minimal makeup enhanced her beauty. She looked twenty years younger, easily.

"What's the matter, girls? You didn't know I was this hot, eh?" Gertie laughed. "Sixty years wheeling yourself around, and you can have arms like these too!"

"You're stunning, Gertie," Veronica said, blown away by how beautiful and young her employer looked.

"I agree!" Tanner chimed in, obviously smitten.

"Gertie, the table you requested is all set." Harper pointed to a table in the rear of the room. It was dressed like the rest of the tables, but was reserved for a few employees. Gertie, Harper, Ben, and Veronica would sit there, apparently Tanner was Gertie's date. Veronica still couldn't wrap her head around that, but her dismay at Gertie's choice of plus-one was over-shadowed by the fact that one person was missing—TJ.

"Thank you, dear. It's show time, everyone! Enjoy yourselves, but more importantly, make sure our guests enjoy themselves more!" Gertie yelled to all the servers hustling around the room.

Veronica scanned the room, telling herself that she was making sure everything was in place. She was not searching for TJ. Nope. She hadn't seen or heard from him since they had put the tent back up a few days ago. She figured he was avoiding her because she'd assumed the worst of him when she'd seen him kiss Sarah. Her heart sank, and she took her seat just as the wedding party arrived at the door.

The lead singer of the Frank Sinatra-style band took the mic. "Ladies and gentlemen, please stand as we welcome Mr. and Mrs. Jasper Kenney!"

The ballroom exploded with applause as Jasper and Marly entered and walked toward the dance floor for their first dance as husband and wife.

Veronica held her breath as she saw Harper standing off to the side with the box of butterflies.

Please, let this go right!

As the song started, she nodded to Harper, who slowly opened the box. Nothing happened. Harper looked at Veronica with a panicked look on her face. Just as Veronica was about to signal to her to close the box, a single butterfly emerged. It slowly flew toward the couple and then drifted upward, out toward the sky via the open glass wall. Dozens of butterflies followed in hues of gold, purple, and orange, the colors brilliantly vivid from the slanting light of the setting sun.

Veronica let out a huge sigh of relief and sat down at the table. It felt good to get off of her feet, even if only for a minute. She had been running around for hours. Across the table, Gertie and Tanner were engrossed in conversation, their heads bent together. Ugh… what was Gertie thinking?

She scanned the room and spotted Edward at the bar. He looked handsome in his tuxedo. Though Veronica wasn't sure they'd ever be friends, she hoped she'd earned at least a little respect with the way she'd pulled the wedding together. She tried to catch his eye and give him a little finger wave, but he was too busy glaring at Gertie and Tanner. Was he jealous?

Veronica still didn't trust Tanner, but Gertie was a big girl and could pick her own friends. She only hoped Gertie knew what she was doing. Even though

Tanner really had tried to make things right, and he had protected Harper by insisting she had nothing to do with any of his attempts at sabotage, he would have to do a lot more to prove to Veronica that he wasn't the mean bastard he had been.

Then again, hadn't she done some of those mean things right along with him? And deep down, she wasn't a bad person. She'd had good reason to be angry and bitter. Maybe Tanner had had good reason to be angry and bitter too. And maybe Tanner could change, just as she had.

Her gaze fell from Tanner to Marly's mother, who was seated next to the head table. She looked beautiful. Her chemo treatments had stopped a few months ago, and she had worn a scarf while her hair grew back. Today she had a fabulous short, contemporary, spikey hairdo that highlighted the gorgeous silver tones in her hair. And the color was back in her face as well. Marly had told Veronica that her mother's prognosis was excellent, and Veronica was truly happy about that.

The disc jockey called for the bridesmaids and groomsmen to join the new couple on the dance floor. Veronica watched as Sarah and Raffe walked hand in hand. A wave of guilt washed over her at the thoughts of how she'd tried to ruin the cooking contest for them. She was happy to see they were still together, although now that she saw them, she could see their faces were strained, and it looked as if they'd been arguing. Maybe she should do something nice for them to make up for her past actions.

More people got up to dance, filling the dance floor and flowing out into the tent. Even Gertie and Tanner danced, with Edward trying to cut in. Veronica sat at the table alone. As usual. She deserved it. Maybe this was her penance for being so mean most of her adult life. Karma had come around, and there would be no special man in her life. Still, she wished she at least had someone to talk to. Preferably TJ. She'd really liked him. But he wasn't here.

Maybe he wasn't avoiding *her,* though. He'd mentioned before that being around tents made him nervous because of the fire. He had said he wasn't sure he'd attend because of the tent. Yet, he'd rushed in to help get her out when the tent had collapsed, and he'd even helped to put it back up. That had taken guts. Maybe he did care about her a little.

Veronica slumped in her chair as everyone danced. Even Harper had a dance partner, but Veronica sat alone, feeling stupid. She fidgeted with her bracelets, trying to look as if she was keeping busy. She'd never been on a dance floor in her life, aside from walking across this one and once at a cousin's wedding when she was little. But there was no sense in sitting around feeling sorry for herself. Everyone was so happy, and she pulled it all together. That's all that mattered.

She felt the air shift next to her and turned slightly.

"Care to dance?" TJ stood at her elbow in a black suit with crisp white shirt underneath. His tie was a deep purple, something not many men could pull off, but he certainly did. He looked gorgeous. Veronica stared at him, unsure of what to say.

He raised a brow and held his hand out to her. She took it, and he pulled her up, stopping to examine her dress.

"Wow! Um, I… er…Wow! You look great," TJ sputtered as he gawked.

"Oh this old thing?" Veronica laughed as they headed toward the tent.

"Yeah," TJ replied, slowing.

The tent. Veronica knew he must be hesitating because of the tent. Without even thinking, she grabbed his hand and squeezed, a silent sign that everything was okay. She looked up and caught his eye, seeing a flicker of gratefulness and… maybe even something more. TJ smiled and nodded toward the tent. "After you."

They weaved around a few couples and ended up next to Marly and Jasper. Raffe and Sarah were nearby, and Veronica's stomach somersaulted. What would Sarah think of her brother dancing with her archenemy? But instead of shooting daggers at them, Sarah beamed a smile, and Veronica's heart swelled. She doubted she and Sarah would be best buddies, but maybe in time they could be friends.

Her eyes caught Gertie, who was at the edge of the dance floor with Edward and Tanner on either side of her. They appeared to be arguing about who was going to dance with her. Then Gertie broke away from the two men, leaving them arguing as she wheeled to the stone wall overlooking the water, where Harper was lining up paper lanterns.

Everyone moved from the tent to the lawn, oohing and ahhing as the lanterns slowly floated across the water and up toward the sky.

"It's all so gorgeous! Thank you so much!" Marly gushed at Veronica as she and Sarah watched the lanterns.

"I'm so happy this all came together," Veronica said sincerely. TJ squeezed her hand, giving her a shot of confidence. "Thanks for trusting me to do it."

Marly crossed her arms over her chest and turned to Veronica. "Well, I wasn't sure at first, and we did get off to a rocky start, but you did great."

Veronica's heart filled with pride and hope. For the first time, she was genuinely happy for another person without any thoughts of what was in it for her. The old Veronica was gone, and she didn't miss her one bit.

"It's *my* dance," Edward's raised voice filtered over to them, and they turned to see Edward and Tanner on either side of Gertie. Both of their faces were red, and they looked as though they might come to blows. Gertie sat serenely in the middle looking up at them, a twinkle in her eye and her head swiveling from one to the other as they argued.

"No, Edward. You danced with her last. This dance is mine, and besides, I need to consult with Gertie," Tanner's voice was calm, but he had a determined look on his face.

Edward smirked. "Consult? On what?"

"I'm having all my restaurants made disabled-preferred with special seating and other amenities. I need Gertie's input."

Edward clenched his fists at his sides, reminding Veronica of how he was used to calling the shots and getting his own way. "Ha! Well, I need her input more than you!"

"Why is that?"

"*I'm* starting a fashion line for wheelchair users at Draconia, and I need Gertie's assistance!"

Tanner leaned over Gertie, closer to Edward. "Well, *I'm* dancing with her next!"

"Boys, boys!" Gertie waved her hands, pushing them away. "No need to fight. There's plenty of Gertie to go around. But I think I'll sit this one out."

She wheeled out from between them and headed toward Veronica and Marly, shaking her head.

"Well, it looks like you two are getting along much better than you did at that first meeting," Gertie said as she rolled in next to them.

"Yes, Gertie, who would have thought? Somehow you have a way of bringing people together." Marly took Gertie's hand and squeezed it.

"Not me! But, it's a good thing you are together because you may need to get along a lot better in the very near future." Gertie winked at them and wheeled off.

Veronica and Marly exchanged puzzled looks. "Wait! Gertie, what are you talking about?"

Gertie spun her chair at the edge of the dance floor. "Can't talk about it now, but you'll find out soon!"

Then she spun back onto the floor and wheeled off with Edward and Tanner jockeying for position behind her.

Veronica glanced up at TJ. "Do you know what she's talking about?"

TJ shook his head. "No idea, but you know Gertie. She always has something up her sleeve."

Jasper joined them, slipping his arm around Marly and tucking her into his side. Their obvious happiness together made Veronica wish for the same thing. Would that ever happen for her?

The old Veronica's destructive attitude had poisoned every relationship she'd ever had. But now things were looking up for the new Veronica. She'd befriended Harper, even though she wasn't sure she trusted her, and it seemed she might become friends with Marly too.

She glanced up at the handsome guy beside her. He was still holding her hand and standing next to her as though he actually wanted to be there instead of running in the opposite direction.

She'd been happier than she'd ever been working at creating this beautiful wedding for Marly instead of trying to ruin things for everyone around her. Everything had changed and, for the first time in her life, she had hope for a happy future.

****

Join my email list and receive emails about my latest book releases - don't miss out on early release discount on the next book in this series: http://www.leighanndobbs.com/leighann-dobbs-romantic-comedy/

If you want to receive a text message on your cell phone for new releases, text ROMANCE to 88202 (sorry, this only works for US cell phones!)

Join my Facebook Readers group and get special content and the inside scoop on my books: https://www.facebook.com/groups/ldobbsreaders

Other Books in This series:

In Over Her Head (book 1)
Can't Stand the Heat (book 2)

Sweet Romance (Written As Annie Dobbs)

Firefly Inn Series

***

Another Chance (Book 1)

Another Wish (Book 2)

Romantic Cozy Mystery

Blackmoore Sisters

Cozy Mystery Series

* * *

Dead Wrong

Dead & Buried

Dead Tide

Buried Secrets

Deadly Intentions

A Grave Mistake

Spell Found

Fatal Fortune

Silver Hollow

Paranormal Cozy Mystery Series

***

A Spell of Trouble (Book 1)

Spell Disaster (Book 2)

Nothing to Croak About (Book 3)

Cry Wolf (Book 4)

Cozy Mysteries

Lexy Baker Cozy Mystery Series

* * *

Lexy Baker Cozy Mystery Series Boxed Set Vol 1 (Books 1-4)

Or buy the books separately:

Killer Cupcakes

Dying For Danish

Murder, Money and Marzipan

3 Bodies and a Biscotti

Brownies, Bodies & Bad Guys

Bake, Battle & Roll

Wedded Blintz

Scones, Skulls & Scams

Ice Cream Murder

Mummified Meringues

Brutal Brulee (Novella)

No Scone Unturned

Cream Puff Killer

Mooseamuck Island Cozy Mystery Series

* * *

A Zen For Murder

A Crabby Killer

A Treacherous Treasure

Mystic Notch

Cat Cozy Mystery Series

* * *

Ghostly Paws

A Spirited Tail

A Mew To A Kill

Paws and Effect

Probable Paws

Kate Diamond Mystery Adventure Series

Hidden Agemda (book 1)

Ancient Hiss Story (book 2)

***

Hazel Martin Historical Mystery Series

***

Murder at Lowry House (book 1)

Murder by Misunderstanding (book 2)

Regency Matchmaker Mysteries

***

An Invitation to Murder (Book 1)

Sam Mason Mysteries

(As L. A. Dobbs)

***

Telling Lies (Book 1)

Keeping Secrets (Book 2)

Exposing Truths (Book 3)

Regency Romance

* * *

Scandals and Spies Series:

Kissing The Enemy

Deceiving the Duke

Tempting the Rival

Charming the Spy

Pursuing the Traitor

_____

ABOUT THE AUTHOR

USA Today Bestselling author Leighann Dobbs has had a passion for reading since she was old enough to hold a book, but she didn't put pen to paper until much later in life. After a twenty-year career as a software engineer with a few side trips into selling antiques and making jewelry, she realized you can't make a living reading books, so she tried her hand at writing them and discovered she had a passion for that, too! She lives in New Hampshire with her husband, Bruce, their trusty Chihuahua mix, Mojo, and beautiful rescue cat, Kitty.

Her book "Dead Wrong" won the "Best Mystery Romance" award at the 2014 Indie Romance Convention.

Her book "Ghostly Paws" was the 2015 Chanticleer Mystery & Mayhem First Place category winner in the Animal Mystery category.

Don't miss out on the early buyers discount on Leighann's next cozy mystery - signup for email notifications:

http://www.leighanndobbs.com/newsletter

Want text alerts for new releases? TEXT alert straight on your cellphone. Just text COZYMYSTERY to 88202

(sorry, this only works for US cell phones!)

Connect with Leighann on Facebook:

http://facebook.com/leighanndobbsbooks

Join her VIP Readers group on Facebook:

https://www.facebook.com/groups/ldobbsreaders

Printed in Great Britain
by Amazon

40751706R00129